FRENCH FOR DI
GAME ON/FAITES
BY CARYS M.

TABLE OF CONTENTS

PROLOGUE

CHAPTER 1

CHAPTER 2

CHAPTER 3

CHAPTER 4

CHAPTER 5

CHAPTER 6

CHAPTER 7

CHAPTER 8

CHAPTER 9

CHAPTER 10

CHAPTER 11

CHAPTER 12

CHAPTER 13

CHAPTER 14

CHAPTER 15

CHAPTER 16

CHAPTER 17

CHAPTER 18

CHAPTER 19

CHAPTER 20

CHAPTER 21

CHAPTER 22

CHAPTER 23

CHAPTER 24

I dad

CHAPTER 25

CHAPTER 26

CHAPTER 27

CHAPTER 28

CHAPTER 29

CHAPTER 30

CHAPTER 31

CHAPTER 32

CHAPTER 33

CHAPTER 34

CHAPTER 35

CHAPTER 36

CHAPTER 37

CHAPTER 38

CHAPTER 39

CHAPTER 40

CHAPTER 41

CHAPTER 42

CHAPTER 43

EPILOGUE

PROLOGUE

"Italy's not bad," said Dutch Famke.

"Sweden gets my vote," gushed Giulia.

"*Null point* for Luxembourg though," scorned Céline. "He hasn't looked over once."

This is my kind of Eurovision, thought Catherine on the first night of her student exchange programme in Germany as she sat there in front of a *Bier*, checking out the talent with an eclectic bunch of fellow-students from all over the continent. Induction night at the campus bar was like opening a chocolate assortment box on Christmas morning … and they weren't selecting their course modules.

"Not quite the 'Luxury Collection' though is it," pointed out Jenny, being a bit of a wet blanket. But then, she had a boyfriend back at university in England and the 'year out' for her was tainted by concerns about whether long-distance love could go the distance.

For Catherine, on the other hand, the year-out held the heady promise of excitement and romance, new beginnings and possibilities. It was 1992. It was all about Maastricht and European Union, exchange programmes and oysters lying open to be downed like shots at a vodka bar, and she was going to be living the European dream for the next ten months.

"Catherine," whispered Céline, pronouncing it the French way, turning the soft 'th' into a sharp 't', "I know my own countrymen, and I think France is making ze flirt wiz you. He has not stopped looking on you since we walked in."

"I'm here to study German literature not French Lotharios," said Catherine, but looked back over her shoulder just in case.

A bad move, as anyone who's studied their Classics will know.

CHAPTER 1

There had to be a way. A solution to keep it all together. To prevent it all from coming tumbling down. To make a sense of the tangled web. To contain the mess. To bring it all to an ordered conclusion. Preferably one where she came out the winner. It couldn't be that difficult putting some method into the madness.

She analysed it from every angle. Moved around the stacked maze of difficulty. Thinking that she had struck on a way out, at the last minute she realised that it would be a fatal unravelling. It would set off a chain reaction of events.

The others were starting to become restless, egging her on, daring her to take the risk and bare her strategy. She bowed to the pressure and applied all her dexterity to keeping the precarious whole afloat while extricating the vassal from the rule of the emperor. Bad move. The empire collapsed, scattering parts in every direction, joining the already fallen needles under the Christmas tree and then taking cover under the scraggy tufts of the designer rug.

"My turn *maman*," shrieked Manon, before grabbing up the easy pickings of the Mikado sticks strewn across, beneath and around the French oak table and the colourful spectrum of industrial-look metal chairs, finishing the game before her brother got a look-in.

Sensing the looming war that would inevitably end with two Mikado sticks split in half by a frenzied duel, a couple consumed in the fireplace and another up a nostril or plunged into an eye, followed by a night-time visit to the Accident and Emergency Department,

Catherine announced that hot chocolate with Chantilly cream was up next before bedtime.

"Will *papa* be back before we go to bed?" asked Arthur as he followed her into the French country style kitchen, the one that made all her old friends back home in Wales believe that her life was just one long year in Provence with a soundtrack of crickets and Edith Piaf, even though her home was 3 hours north of *Pastis* country and 4 hours south of *Pigalle*.

'*Papa,*' she mused.

It still made her smile to think that the guy in the Bierkeller had gradually been promoted from the 'Frenchie', to Jacques, to her *fiancé*, to her *époux* and then *papa*, twice, and taken her from posting to posting until they'd settled in a corner of France that was two hours by train from the 3 Ps central to French life: the fashionista heaven of *Paris*, the sweet saltiness of the *Plage* and the frosted delight of the *Pistes*.

Brought back from her walk down memory lane by a tug on her skirt, she looked down at her son.

"I doubt it darling. He called me earlier to say that his plane was delayed. He may not even make it back to St Desirée tonight."

Arthur immediately hunched his shoulders and crossed his arms in a way that, in a few years' time, would qualify for him for membership of a dodgy French hip-hop band. Catherine, desperate to jump in just in time to avoid any such Justin Babyerish developments, immediately comforted him.

"Oh don't be upset darling, this Polish business trip is just a bit longer than usual. Come on, big strong seven-year olds like you don't cry. You are half Welsh you know!"

"He will be back for Christmas though, won't he?" Manon asked worriedly.

Time for a sprinkling of seasonal white lies, Catherine thought.

"Of course! He was just up in Lapland last week checking that Father Christmas was up to date with his Christmas schedule."

Arthur's eyes opened in wonder.

"Is that why he travels so much? Does he work for *Papa Noël*?"

Seeing the hope rekindle behind the cynicism that had started to dim the innocence in Manon's nine-year old eyes, she crouched down conspiratorially beside them, put an arm around two slight shoulders and whispered in her ear.

"Let's just say that elf management is something he used to do and that dealing with presents and lots of white stuff is part of his job description."

In adult terms, this meant that he used to be in the oil business but was now in the much less glamorous but surprisingly lucrative world of international toilet paper sales.

Disasters deflected and fears allayed, after a well-deserved kiss and a cuddle Catherine finally closed the bedroom doors on another day of parenting, or as it often felt like, single-parenting, and headed back down to what the day had left to offer her.

The dreaded task lay ahead, the one that blighted the run-up to Christmas every year. It was a burden worse than finding a present for the mother-in-law who had everything and valued nothing for the

15th year running without repeating herself, more nerve-wracking than untangling Christmas lights that seemed to have been playing Twister to keep themselves busy since last January, and even more challenging than making up excuses to the children for their father's absence, yet again, from the Christmas concert.

She took a detour through that much-envied kitchen on a search for some motivation in the oversized American fridge and found a half-finished champagne bottle with a spoon dangling down its neck. The fleeting thought rushed as always through her mind that she really should ask someone one day to explain the spoon and bubble theory to her. Did it actually work? Did the piece of metal really keep the wine from getting flat? Or was it just a suburban myth? Not that it mattered, seeing that not many bottles of champagne were abandoned in her fridge once opened.

Effortlessly moving on from that existentialist concern, she grabbed her 'motivation' and an exquisite blue Baccarat wineglass that had miraculously survived from the pile of wedding gifts through all those dinner parties and house moves between international postings, and collapsed onto the sofa.

She looked around her living room. The Christmas tree shimmered like something out of the *Printemps* department store's Christmas window, an early snow shower outside was promising good skiing conditions for the New Year break to the Alps, her own face looked back at her from the back cover of her first novel that adorned one of the many bookshelves, as always making her feel rather bemused, like the twin sister of a more successful sibling, and her children beamed back at her in their swimming costumes from the framed photos of last summer's Mediterranean holiday. In another photo, she was smiling at Jacques while he gazed wistfully into the distance. Probably thinking of work again. She raised her glass to the photo. "*Santé* hubby, wherever you are tonight."

"Right, can't put it off any longer."

Putting down her liquid incentive, she grabbed the laptop pricking her conscience on the coffee table, waited for it to whir into life and embarked on the annual chore.

To:	Undisclosed recipients
Re:	Christmas Greetings from the Duponts!

Hi lovely friends and family,

We're finally going fir-tree green this year and saving the planet by giving up that barbaric tradition of paper Christmas cards! All karma for the year ahead, and anyway, champagne doesn't taste quite the same after licking all those stamps!

Everything is great in France. Jacques is busy as usual with his work, travelling the planet on his business trips without any time to see anything of the world, poor thing. I'm still working hard on my next novel, battling writer's block and the urge to open the fridge door.

The children are absolutely thriving at their international school. Manon is already nine and Arthur is hitting seven soon ... which reminds me, keep your dates free for my 40th in two years' time! We'll have to jet you all in from the four corners of the globe. *C'est fantastique* this international life! But what would we do without all this electronic communication, this tangled but intriguing web of friendship we weave between our Google-earthed homes and our Facebooked facades... but that's just me twittering on again. LOL.

All our love and best wishes for the new year from the Dupont family! *Vive la France!*

Catherine, Jacques, Manon and Arthur

Heaving a sigh of relief as the mail careered through space to places that, in some cases she had never seen, and to people who, in some cases, she had never really known ... and in other cases, never really liked, she switched on the TV. The most exciting programme on was a documentary about political revolutions, so she decided to get ready for bed and watch what was going on in the outside world from inside her cocoon.

Going into Supermum mode, that most under-revered and over-looked of superheroes, she emptied the dishwasher with the speed and accuracy of a circus knife-thrower, sorted the clothes in the laundry room with the logistical mind of an automated picker, added the final touches to a school show costume with the skill of a Dior seamstress, checked on the kids, brushed her teeth and applied her face cream with circular movements with one hand while checking all the doors and windows with the other. She then fell into bed, fumbled for the remote control under the covers, the only action they would see that night, and switched on the French news.

All the news channels seemed to be running with the same breaking story, a televised announcement by the French President. Catherine fought against the drowsiness brought on by the long day and the evanescent champagne dregs and sat up. What was it going to be this time? Another ministerial reshuffle to bring in a past sports champion to secure the next Olympics for Paris? A hijacked pensioner saved from his captors after being stumbled upon by the French army in the African desert during their search for nimble Nigerian schoolgirls? Oh God, was the legendary French rock singer Johnny "I pretend I'm American" Halliday dead?

She turned up the volume to see what the ridiculous little fellow had to say.

"Citizens, I am addressing you exceptionally tonight to put an end to the rumours and claims circulating in the press with the sole intention of ensuring that focus remains on my work as your

President and of allowing me to fulfil my duty to my country. I have today settled matters relating to my personal life. I will be the sole occupant of the Elysée Palace from now on and will carry out all official duties as a single man. The person concerned has been duly notified. That is all I have to say. *Vive la France.*"

Oh la la! He'd given the First Lady the chuck! Well to be precise, she was only the First Girlfriend given that they weren't married, or even bound by a civil partnership, in fact she was just the bit on the side. So all those press rumours were true, he did have a bit on the side of the bit on the side! In that noble French tradition, the ruler was having his cake and eating it. Where did they find the time?

Catherine's musings were interrupted by an interview a journalist was holding with a French MP. Pouncing on him as he was making his way out of the Party offices he hurled his question at him.

"Monsieur Toussaint, could you just tell me what the general reaction is to the President's personal life within the Party?"

The answer came like a shot, none of that looking shame-faced and mumbling about family values. *Au diable* with that, Monsieur Toussaint was clearly treading the Party line.

"What do we think about the President's personal life? Exactly that, it's personal. We care only about his politics. Whether he has a mistress, or two of them, we don't care, as long as he heads up the country. Come on, this is France. It's hardly news is it? *C'est la vie!*"

Catherine had lived on and off in *la belle France* for the past eleven years, since marrying the French lothario she had first met in that *Bierkeller*. She genuinely liked the place. The countryside was beautiful, eating was a national sport, childcare was cheap and State-sponsored and you could still criticise screw-top wine bottles without being considered a wine snob, but there were times when she felt that she would never get to grips with the country.

She stared in disbelief at this farcical display of old boys' club behaviour and found herself muttering out loud.

"I think they've just institutionalised infidelity. They've enshrined it in the Constitution as freedom of sexpression. Next time they mention a cabinet reshuffle I'm just going to have visions of a ministerial gang bang. Poor thing, being dumped on television, in public like that is just so callous. What a cad. It's worse than reality TV."

Exhausted by this unexpected outburst of disapproval at her adopted country, Catherine turned to switch off the light. The framed photograph of her husband on her bedside table reminded her that, thankfully there were exceptions to the rule, and she didn't even have to revert to the good old Welsh tradition of counting sheep to fall into Morpheus' arms, as the French so poetically put it. Not that she had much choice, the God of dreams was the only one who was there to hold her close that night, and most nights at the moment.

CHAPTER 2

Six months later

It was one of those summer nights on which you could actually use the word balmy. None of those Northern European chilly breezes that had you rushing in for your cardigan and your hand hovering for a reckless moment above the tights drawer, and none of that Southern European sauna-like excess that caused tears to trickle down from the backs of your knees, desperate to find relief from your overheated body. It was fair, temperate, clement. Nature's scales in perfect balance.

It was also almost the end of the French working year. June in France was a preview of the two-month long summer holiday ahead. It was spent preparing children in swimming pools for the joys of the waves to the West or South, tasting rosés to free the mind for other concerns, such as *boules* or the *Tour de France* once the summer officially began, and winding up projects or shelving others to clear the desk for the unadulterated enjoyment of *les grandes vacances*.

And so it was that on one such balmy summer night in June Jacques seemed to be engrossed in the latter endeavour, working hard on his laptop on the terrace to make space for the family time he had promised his family that summer.

It had all started well, as only that evening they had dined al fresco at their favourite local restaurant to celebrate Manon's birthday. So well, in fact, that Catherine had only had to ask Jacques to put down his smartphone and listen to the children three times in the course of the entire evening, although he had spent quite a while on it when he went to the bathroom or to fetch a forgotten wallet from the car.

Catherine had gone to bed but was wearing one of her slinky lingerie numbers and, though their mother tongues may not have been the same, there was no need for an interpreter to tell him what that meant. She was waiting for him. He supposed she deserved it. Actually maybe she needed it, he thought to himself, having lost her dad only a few weeks ago to a long illness. It had been a tough few months for her watching him slowly fade from her life picture. But just as he was about to switch off his laptop and go to avail himself of his spousal duties he heard that familiar Skype call coming in.

He smiled when he saw who was calling and quickly answered.

"Just wait two seconds, I need to check something," he said, before heading off towards the bedroom.

Giving Catherine a quick peck on the cheek and mumbling something about sales figures, he hoofed it back to the deck area outside, careful to shut the door on the way.

He paused at the doorway to watch unobserved the face that seemed to be searching the surroundings through the glass button of the webcam. She looked like someone looking through a keyhole for a glimpse of what lay on the other side, or, he uncomfortably felt, looking into a crystal ball to see what the future may hold in store for her if she played her cards right.

Shutting the glass door behind him, he caught a quick glance of his own reflection. What he saw was a man a good ten years older, but not necessarily wiser, than the blonde-haired marketing assistant who was doing extra hours tonight by calling him at this time.

"What took you so long? It's almost midnight," she scolded in an accent containing the steely remnants of Solidarnosc, as he came into her view in front of the computer.

"I told you earlier, I just had to deal with some family stuff," he replied.

She pouted in commiseration at his tough life.

"Poor you." she purred.

Basking in this unconditional understanding emanating from the line-free innocence of the angelic face, he moved into the screen.

"Oh my God I miss you so much… and now I have the summer holidays to get through."

The purring veered into a slight petulance at the thought that the screen was not the only thing between them.

"Can't you make up some urgent business? Get away from them? And come to me?"

The firmness started to leave his backbone and slide mindlessly down his body as he felt himself caving in.

"I could I suppose… I'll just send them to the beach house on the Med as usual. It won't be too difficult making up an excuse to get away for a few days. She trusts me completely. God knows why! Bit naïve for such an intelligent woman … Oh *merde*!"

A dark cloud passed over the girl's skype-blue eyes that started to scrutinise the screen in panic.

"Darling, darling, what is happening? I can hear noises … I'm losing you."

The screen went black as the computer screen was pushed down by a male hand.

***

Catherine made a grab for the computer and brandished it in the air with a threat. "Who is she? Who the hell is the bitch? I want to know. How long has it been going on? I can't believe this. I can't believe this is happening to me? Answer me!"

Not daring to look his wife in the eyes and keeping them riveted on the computer that was too far off the ground to hope for any soft landing, Jacques went for denial. "I told you I was looking over some figures with a colleague."

"Looking a colleague's figure over more like it! Don't lie to me!"

The arm holding the computer edged backwards to gain momentum but Jacques made a grab for it and held it in front of his chest like a bullet proof vest. Not a bad move, as Catherine darted to the barbecue to snatch a pair of sharp utensils and, with Zorroesque flair, forced Jacques to step backwards away from the charcoal-blackened forks until he was tripped up and entrapped by the Adirondack.

"Don't lie to me," she hysterically repeated. "It's midnight. We've just spent the evening as a family. I was waiting for you in bed. You bastard. I thought you'd want to round off the evening making love to your wife but no you have better plans, Skypesex with your mistress? Who the hell is she?"

Crazed with anger and disbelief, Catherine had been prodding him with increasing force with the fork. The whole scene could have been out of a torture scene from a Guantanamo prison riot on barbecue night. Jacques tried his best to reason to the good cop lying within.

"Can you just calm down a bit? I won't say anything if you keep on coming at me with that thing."

Unfortunately for him, bad cop was on duty that night.

"Calm down!!" Catherine had clearly ditched the literary intellectual image she had opted for on the book cover and gone for the Sarah Connor vibe as she grabbed another Adirondack and threw it into the swimming pool. "You want me to calm down? So tell me, how am I supposed to react? Like a good French wife? Ask you if she wants to join us for a ménage à trois then go back to reading bloody Elle?"

She hit his legs with the rusty spatula she was brandishing as a subtle hint that he may like to come out with something more than obvious lies.

"Ok, she's a girl from work."

It was a beginning, but then Catherine could have first guessed that one.

"How original. How long?"

Hesitating for just a fraction of a second too long, Catherine came at him again, this time with tongs, like some redneck Samurai.

"How long?"

Too cowardly to risk another utensil-inflicted wound he quietly mouthed the answer.

"About a year."

Catherine dropped her weapons, stepping back as if struck by the confession.

"A year, a year. Where? Who is she? Is she French?"

"No."

"English?"

"No."

"German?"

"No."

Catherine saw herself having to go through the entire European bloody Union and then the United Nations so cut to the chase.

"Where does she live?"

Jacques sensed that he would have to give her some more if he had any chance of escape or even of escaping with his life.

"*D'accord, d'accord*, she's Polish. I met her at a conference. It's not as if I've got some "*garçonniere*" where I go for an afterwork every day."

Catherine couldn't believe the cheek of him, had flashbacks to that Presidential broadcast and realised that the *exception française* did not apply to her husband after all.

"Oh good for you, does that constitute fidelity in France? Is that your way of saying you love me? By not having a regular mistress on my doorstep where you can go for happy hour? But hey if you're dipping your prick in cabbage soup abroad that doesn't count does it? What do you do? Decontaminate yourself with potato vodka before catching the plane home? A year! At least that's what you're admitting to."

Jacques turned an even darker hue of red.

"Come on Catherine. Don't take it that way, listen to me *chérie*."

It wasn't the right thing to say. There probably wasn't a right thing to say. But it certainly wasn't that. Catherine calmly picked up the fallen utensils, and her eyes glazed over as she started to unconsciously execute sharpening movements with them.

"Don't take it that way? I came back from my father's funeral two weeks ago you bastard."

Jacques bowed his head and Catherine knew that the meat was "*au point*", that if she stuck in the knife now all the bloody juice would seep out.

"It wasn't work you had to rush back to was it?"

An almost inaudible "no" could be heard above the crickets.

What Catherine said next came out in the same hushed tones but were tinged with wrath not shame.

"Get out of my house. Get out of here. I never want to see you again. Get out. Get the hell out of here."

But the rasping gradually crescendoed into a volcanic finale.

"Just go. Now. Go. Go. Go."

Before Jacques could respond or move, a noise coming from the house brought the gladiators out from the arena they had built around themselves. Their sparring had attracted an audience, an unwelcome one. Their children, the dual nationality offspring of their cross-border union, were standing at the open patio doors in their pyjamas, a look of fear and bewilderment filling their beautiful faces.

"*Maman, papa*, we're scared," said Manon, who, as the eldest, had clearly been given the role of official spokesperson.

Emboldened by his sister's initiative, Arthur took a step outside.

"Why is papa going? Where is he going?"

Catherine divested herself quickly of her culinary weapons but could come up with nothing better than a weak joke.

"I was just giving your father a grilling."

Ignoring this pitiful attempt at an explanation, the children tried to struggle their way around Catherine who had by now come towards them and was trying to take them inside. Jacques was still sitting on the garden chair with his head in his hands, unable to face them.

"But what has *papa* done *maman*?"

Catherine knelt down in front of Arthur.

"He's been a naughty boy darling. He's just been a very naughty boy and done lots of very silly things. Come on in, you'll freeze."

"But *papa's* going to be cold outside," piped up Manon, filial love finding its level as it is want to do.

But something in Catherine had broken. Nature may abhor a vacuum but all she could feel was a growing void where her heart had once been.

"Oh don't worry about *papa* darling. *Papa* always finds a way of coming in from the cold."

She looked around at the dejected and hunched figure and, her voice cracking, hissed her hate at him.

"*Casse-toi pauvre con.*"

CHAPTER 3

By the time she had settled the children again, making the most of her talent for fiction to convince them that she was only angry with their father because he had to leave again urgently on business, the balmy night had ebbed into the darkest hour.

All of her emotions were on overdrive. She felt like a cornered animal, all senses on alert, subjected to such cruelty that it was ready to defend itself at all costs. She sat there in the unlit living room listening for any signs that Jacques could still be out there in the garden and scanning the house with her eyes for any clues that could have told her this was about to happen.

That was when she felt it. The tingle of disgust washed over her skin. It felt like a tsunami that slowly dragged every cell with it as it stripped her body of any outer protection before concentrating every inch of her being in her stomach. She thankfully made it to the bathroom before the seismic wave of bile was unleashed with its corpses of memories and thick debris of anger and hurt.

She sat on the shower floor for a long time, how long she didn't know, rubbing, scouring, pleading with the contaminated skin to leave her body and washing herself over and over again. It was probably the most ineffective shower ever as her salty tears mingled with the mains water and her howling was drowned out only by the gushing flow.

Getting him out of her skin and her out of her mind would take longer she imagined.

Her hair still streaming water, she dried herself off summarily and sat on her bed, hugging her knees. The hollow created by the punch, the one she hadn't seen coming, was slowly starting to be filled with questions. How had she been so blind? Did their friends know? Who was the girl? Why didn't he love her anymore? Why? Why? Why? And, more pressingly maybe, what was she going to do now?

Sleep not being something she could contemplate for the next year or so she decided that action was the only option open to her. With methodical, clinical calm, powered by a burning anger, she got to work.

His ties were easy prey. She took the kitchen scissors and made light work of cutting them all in half, imagining with each snip the thin strips of Hugo Boss or Burberry interspersed by Tie Rack and good old Marks & Spencer being used by a Polish blond to tie Jacques to a hotel bed.

His shoes were also an easy picking as she filled the foppish Italian brands with shaving foam and had visions of Jacques enjoying Champagne-drenched romantic dinners in foreign destinations as she did the kids' homework.

Doing that only strengthened her resolve and she got started on the task of stuffing all his clothes into bin bags and throwing them gleefully into the garden. With each bag she counted the weekends when he'd "been attending conferences" or "lost flights" in the past year.

She had one thing left to do on her unplanned schedule of revenge. She knew that it wasn't a bin bag that could easily be recovered or a tie that could be replaced. It wasn't a shoe that could be dried out.

Without being permanent, going through with it meant that she was stepping onto the path of no return. It was as definitive as you could get in today's world.

She went to the laptop, logged on and with a few clicks she told the world that she was "single" and no longer "married". She saved the profile change and sat there looking at the screen, the shock of what was happening and what she had just done setting in. A bell tinkled, telling her that it was too late to change it back anyway and she stared as one, two and then three new notifications sounded the death knell for her marriage.

"Hey, do you know what time it is over there! Just seen your status change. What's going on?"

The next was a less curious "????", as if she'd just had a moment of madness.

"Everything ok?" showed a bit more concern while "LOL" seemed to think that she was one hell of a funny woman.

"Did you press the wrong button or what?" just saw her as an idiot.

"As if" was an unbeliever.

"WTF!" would have sworn they were the perfect couple and "Husband away on business again?" was firmly convinced that they were.

"You've got me worried Catherine. What's happening? Can I call?" was probably the most sincere.

The growing number of comments threw Catherine into a panic. She had thought she had a few hours to know herself what was going on before she had to face the world. But now she had set the ball in motion and would have to roll with it. But before that she would have to write the story for the rest of her life, the one she had thought was already nicely typed out, formatted and filed.

She went back to the bedroom, picking up a bottle of vodka on the way for inspiration.

CHAPTER 4

Her water bill was going to be huge, Catherine thought, as she sat there again huddled on the floor in the corner of the walk-in shower. She thought of just filling the bath with cold water and sitting in it. Maybe it would numb the pain. Cryotherapy was probably the way to go. This crying therapy wasn't making her feel any better anyway.

She looked down at her body, disgusted at what she saw. She hated the fact that her feet hadn't seen a pedicurist since … well never actually. She was more of the walking barefoot until your feet can walk over burning coals type. She worked her way up, critically contemplating the translucent roadmaps of varicose veins and the contour lines of her stretch marks that had seen mountains grow and fall in an accelerated version of the world's creation. Her chest wasn't bad for a 38-year-old with two children, for God's sake it was Himalayan at least in this country that barely hit 34 A on the Brassière scale.

But clearly this trodden ground with its vestiges of history was now a heritage site and any developments were being planned for pastures new. She started the rubbing again until the loofah turned the white plains into scorched earth.

She could have sat there for days on end. Her energy had been sapped by the previous night's revelations and the lack of sleep. The vodka had bought her only an hour or so of unconsciousness and left her paying the price.

A bang on the bathroom door forced her to switch off the water. It was Manon telling her that there was someone on the phone for her.

She got up, picked up a towel and looked at herself in the mirror.

"Tell them I'll give them a ring back."

She started laughing hysterically as she looked at her fingers. She slowly pulled off her engagement ring, followed by her wedding ring. The marks they left seemed to be as tangible as the defiled noble metals themselves. Lifting the toilet seat cover she was about to throw them in but changed her mind and opened the bathroom door. Her daughter was still there, the phone in her hand. She took it from her and, in exchange, gave her the gleaming stones.

"Here darling, something for you to play with. That's all they seem to be good for."

Manon looked in awe at the diamonds and then at her mother as she walked down the hall. The same mummy but somehow different. She couldn't say what but something told her that this wasn't a good time to ask her to play mummies and daddies with her in the playhouse in the garden.

Catherine pressed the red button without even looking who the caller could have been. Instead she changed the voicemail message.

"Jacques Dupont is out of his marriage and will never be back. For any urgent matters, please contact his mistress."

On automatic pilot she took the children downstairs to have their breakfast and told them they could watch TV as she had something important to do. Puffy eyed from last night's drama they were happy to obey such an order and picked up their comforters on the way to the TV room.

As soon as they were out of the way, Catherine was back in the office, carefully closing the door behind her. She had to know more. Who was the girl who had revolutionised her world overnight? What did she look like? What was she like? What did she have that she didn't? Again she took her grievances to the lucky dip of the web, knowing that if she delved a little into its depths, it could reveal a multitude of secrets. She could touch on something that might make a mess all around her and leave her with a lot of cleaning up to do, but she would have to risk it.

She had no name, no address, no details so her first stop was her husband's corporate website. She trawled through the country contacts, the organisation charts, the photos on the news pages but there was no sign of a young blond marketing assistant. As she came to the bottom of the news page she saw something that could carry a clue. It was a video from last year's annual conference, the one in Germany he'd had to rush back early from the Easter holidays to attend. In a few clicks she was looking at it. All that was missing was the popcorn.

Jacques Dupont, her husband in name only, was giving a PowerPoint presentation, being witty and charming, to go by the smiles, in front of a conference room audience. She turned up the volume to hear what he was saying.

> "We all know, and nobody knows it
> better than CleanCul, that shit happens.
> (titters from audience) It's true that our
> customers are sitting ducks ... we could

almost call them toilet ducks (titters) but the latest sales figures will wipe the smile off your face, as CleanCul needs to get off its arse if it doesn't want to go down the drain. And I'm sure she won't mind if I say what prettier arse than that of Maria's to break down these figures for us, leaf by leaf!"

Feeling like a reverse fortune teller, Catherine painfully looked on as Maria, clearly the woman she had glimpsed on her husband's computer no more than 12 hours ago, mounted the podium, shared a wink and smile with Jacques and started to strut her stuff.

She couldn't believe how easy it had been, no hacking, no Googling, it was just there, as if his company was meeting its transparency obligations. Was that corporate social responsibility these days? Not hiding internal employee flings from the external stakeholders back home?

Knowing that more secrets could be coaxed out with the right caressing of the keyboard, Catherine spent the next few hours doing what she usually hated, auditing their bank accounts and phone bills with the same frenzy as Behring's Bank's chartered accountant when the figures first failed to add up.

It was all there, the almost predictable Cartier jewellery, the almost unbearable Victoria's Secret underwear and the sheer blatancy of the calls with the Polish country code.

She had one thing left to do on this Saturday morning shopping spree where the computer was doing all the shopping and she all the adding up. Now she could put a face to a name. She typed it into the rather unfortunately named "Find friends" box and came face to face with her rival. Oh for God's sake, the girl was doing a sexy selfie in knickers as a profile photo.

She didn't know who to be most disgusted at, her husband for going for that kind of girl, or herself for going for that kind of husband. Again she felt that urge to shed her skin, that skin that had been cross-contaminated by his enthusiastic pollinating.

Catherine angrily pushed down the Mac book cover and stared at it for a minute. "Mac the Knife. Bloody accessory to the facts."

Another thought then struck her and she cranked it open again. She had just about time to type in "HIV tests" "laboratories in France" before returning to hug the cool porcelain of her new BFF.

CHAPTER 5

Thank God the medical laboratory had a carpark, thought Catherine to herself as she reversed into one of the many parking spaces. Today she couldn't have handled the stress of parallel parking although she was a nifty parker in normal times.

Years of living up in the French capital before the children were born had made her quite an expert at the "Parisian nudge". This was the art of parking in a space that, to anyone else, would be considered as too small but that could be coaxed into making room for a small city run-about by pinching a rear bumper a few times and rubbing up seductively against an at first reluctant licence plate.

Turning off the engine, she sat there for a while, trying to contain her anger at having to be in this situation and the fear that was paralysing her movements. Being British and not in the habit of keeping people waiting, her sense of propriety expelled her from her hybrid SUV. Keeping on her black sunglasses, those she used to escape from book signings incognito, she walked up the steps and pushed open the clinic's door.

The black sunglasses were not really meant to conceal her identity. After all, the French loved going for medical checks and her visit could have meant a test for anything from allergy to pregnancy. No, her paparazzi-dodging look was more to hide the Longchamp-size bags under her eyes and photoshop-ripe red eyes.

After finishing her barely hushed bitching with her colleague about another colleague's lunch breaks, the receptionist with her sharply bobbed hair and nostrils pinched close by years of being handed sample bottles, deigned to look up at Catherine and didn't fail to take in the roughness. Picking up her social security card with the tip of her fingers she told Catherine to take a seat. The medical biologist would be with her in a minute.

Catherine took a plastic seat in the drab waiting area. A few others were in there with her, grimly looking at the magazines that were still declaring that Carla Bruni was the world's most beautiful First Lady or looking around at the health education posters with slogans such as 'Tell me what your blood's like and I'll tell you what you're like'.

The biologist, a middle-aged man who looked in need of a good testing himself, starting with an alcotest, popped his head around the door in a way that suggested that there was no time for his entire body to make it into the room.

"Mme Dupont, follow me. Let's see what we've got."

Her first thought as he led her to the booth with its padded dentist-style recliner, was that it looked like something that welcomed a death row inmate when the final appeal to the governor had failed. She gulped as he closed the door behind them.

"So been a naughty girl have we?"

Catherine couldn't believe what she had just heard.

"Excuse me?"

Unperturbed, the biologist pushed up her sleeve and seemed to be having a good look at her arm.

"Well no join the dots there."

His hand brushed her breasts as he tied the rubber strip around her arm but too quickly for her to be sure that it was anything but an accident.

"Been passing around too much of something else then. In it goes and out it comes," he continued as he took the blood sample.

Catherine barely noticed the needle prick, the life-size version grabbing all her attention. She was too flabbergasted to say anything. What was the guy insinuating? Or maybe it was her getting the wrong end of the stick, not understanding the finer points of the French language. But there was no shrugging off that sense that she had just been humiliated.

Mistaking her frowning for fear of the results, the white-coated idiot continued "Oh don't worry. You'll know tomorrow and back you go into the big orgy of life."

Before she could defend her honour in any way, the guy patted her on the lower back towards the door and with an afterthought said "Oh, before you go," and pushed his other hand into a big bowl of condoms and forced them on her.

"Take a few of these. On the house."

Marching out before her with the sample, he left her at the door feeling soiled and dirty. No that wasn't quite true, even more soiled and dirty than when she had come in.

In one fell swoop he had turned her from a responsible citizen into a cheap slut. She walked out in a daze, holding the condoms in her hand.

But revenge would be hers. As soon as she stepped outside, she saw her chance. The clinical biologist's car was sitting there in its designated parking space with the pretentious name plaque. It was new, bright and shiny. No one was looking. She walked in its direction and strategically dropped her keys as she passed it. Looking around, she made sure that no one was witness to her sabotage. She picked the bunch of keys up with one hand while stuffing the handful of condoms he had so thoughtfully dealt out to her into his car exhaust. She then calmly got up and smoothed down her short summer dress.

"See how you like that for a blow job," she said, walking away without looking back for a split second, head aloof like the female baddie that has just planted a bomb under James Bond's Aston.

It was too early for a Martini, but feeling shaken and stirred in equal measure she decided that coffee was definitely in order and headed off to find somewhere that would get the blood flowing again after that heart-stopping experience.

***

Back in the empty house the phone rang but quickly went to voicemail, the one Catherine had changed to channel her anger: "Jacques Dupont is out of his marriage and will never be back. For any urgent matters please contact his mistress".

Jacques' exasperation was clear.

"*Putain* Catherine, change this message will you and answer me. We need to talk."

CHAPTER 6

Catherine's mobile was ringing and ringing but the caller clearly wasn't getting the message. She wasn't home to him. She wasn't even having it out with him. She just didn't want to talk to him. She needed time to work her way through her own feelings. Numb and rabid were the two main ones, like a fever that she had to let run its course.

She had questions, a fistful of them and she would have loved nothing more than to beat the answers out of him but the truth was that she was afraid of this stranger that had been living in their house for the last few years.

Her ringing phone was clearly starting to annoy the other customers queuing up for their lattes and smoothies but with one hand holding her laptop and the other her double espresso she had to wait until she found a seat before she could castrate the stalker.

Once she had settled in, plugged in and logged in, she could finally reboot herself with a gulp of the black drug. She hadn't eaten anything much in two days and she felt the caffeine career around her body like a formula one pilot.

Her laptop had served more as spyware than as a working tool for the past two days and she owed an explanation to her editor, who was waiting for a few chapters of her latest thriller. She was about to start typing a mail when she decided to try skyping her, the café being mostly empty and as she started to sense a feeling of loneliness sweeping over her.

She'd regretted her Facebook cry for help because she wasn't ready to receive any at the minute. She hadn't said anything to her mother yet. After all, she was already mourning the loss of her own husband, and she didn't want to upstage her with the loss of hers. She would have told her father, but he was no longer there.

She closed her eyes as the thought of her father submerged all others. While she was yet to make a public announcement, there was one thing that she was even finding hard to admit to herself. But one feeling kept on haunting her. Over and over again. Becoming more real each time.

The scenes of the forced poolside confession swept over her again and she traced back her steps from the deck to the bedroom. Could she trust what she herself had felt that night? She went over the sequence of events in her mind.

She had been lying there, swathed in silk on the bed, as some kind of ridiculous sign to her husband that life went on, even after her father's death, for the sake of the children, for their sake. As she was artfully adjusting the sheets to drape her curves and conceal her cuticle-smeared, hastily varnished toenails, Jacques had come in to say that he would be joining her soon. He'd given no sign that he'd captured the sensual signals, only talked about finishing off some work.

Lying there on her own, the minutes had passed … but that's when Catherine felt something that she couldn't be sure was down to an indistinct earthquake or an other-worldly experience. There was no doubt that she had felt a jolt. It had been like a kick in the behind. A push by an invisible hand. Something had tipped her out of that bed and propelled her out into the garden that night. The problem was that, the more she thought about it, the more certain she was that she didn't live in a seismic part of the world.

Someone had wanted her to learn the truth that night. And she was convinced that it was the hand of god that had helped her catch her husband off-side. The god in question certainly wasn't Apollo but the god of divorce and separation… whoever he or she was. The one that plucked Cupid's arrow from hearts with one merciless wrench, snapping them in two in the process.

This was where things tipped into crazy, hysterical, verge of madness mode, as she harboured a secret certainty that she would never be able to admit to anyone. The hand of god, the guardian angel had a face. A face that she had known all of her life… and she had been mourning for the past month.

From beyond the grave, someone wasn't lying back and letting some idiot make a mockery of his daughter. He had wanted her to know… which also meant that he wanted her to do something about it. He was putting her in a difficult position, making her face up to facts, but, after all, wasn't that what tough love was all about.

She gathered her thoughts, opened her eyes, hoping that she hadn't said anything out loud, so engrossed was she in her supernatural conspiracy theory. It was silly, she knew. It was unmentionable, yes. But still …

The hiss of the percolating coffee brought her down to earth with a bang and she got back to trying to get in touch with people in flesh and blood on the other side …of the Channel, her London editor.

She entered her skype ID and password but hadn't got further than the contacts page when the electronic bleating announced an incoming call. Jacques. She refused his calls. He tried again. Clearly not used to rejection. After the third attempt in a row that was stopping her from establishing her connection, she decided to answer to tell him to leave her alone.

The familiarity of the face was unnerving.

She was about to tell him to stop the conjugal harassment when he stopped her in her tracks with a French perfume-laced mace attack of sentiment.

"*Chèrie*, I don't know if you noticed but today is our 11th wedding anniversary. On this symbolic date, I ask you, I beg you to forgive me and take me back. Let me come home. I love you so much. I will spend the rest of my life making this up to you. I've been under so much pressure over the past few years, the house, the children, the job, the travelling, your novel... I just needed some escape valve ... Please *mon amour ...*"

The attack deserved a vitriol-tipped Swiss-army knife response.

"What a coincidence, isn't the eleventh wedding anniversary the steel wedding anniversary? Why don't you just buy me a knife? I have just the right use for it. Or maybe they've just been spelling it wrong all these years, maybe it was meant to be the "steal anniversary" with an "a", where your husband's mistress steals him away from you. And what do you mean escape valve anyway????!!!! To escape from what? Your beautiful home, stunning children, great friends, faithful wife?"

The war of words continued, one side trying to cajole the other into submission, but prompting the other to only put up her defences.

"Don't be like that, in France, it isn't steel but the "*anniversaire de corail*", coral is surely better than steel …"

"Coral? What's that? Or should I say who's that? Another one of your exotic mistresses? I don't seem to remember you ever taking me to Tahiti to see any real stuff! All those promises! All empty, as empty as our marriage was. I thought we had dreams. I thought we were building something together and yes, it takes effort, yes, it's hard work, yes, it's pressure but I thought we were doing it for us, for the children, for the future. You obviously have no idea what marriage is about. Too much pressure!!! I thought you were a man, not a boy."

"Catherine, my Catherine I beg you, look, I am down on bended knees like that time I asked you to marry me in Vegas. Give us another chance. I want to make this marriage work. You are the woman of my life. No one else counts. It meant nothing, come on, I won't be the first and I won't be the last … It's this damned travelling, being on my own, the mobility, I'll find a job where I'm based nearer to home."

"It's just a pity that your dick wasn't less mobile and based nearer to home. Oh, and you mentioned our engagement in Vegas … I really did bet on the wrong horse. Instead of being your queen of hearts I was just your joker."

"Yes well I'm going to be having the last laugh. Leave me and you'll be on your own. Who wants a middle aged woman with two kids anyway? Your luck has just run out *chérie*. Unfortunately for you, I was your best bet."

The sheer arrogance of the man. Catherine went for her cup and hurled its contents at the face sneering at her on the other side of the screen. Jacques jerked back involuntarily then laughed at her with pity and ended the conversation.

Realising what she had just done, Catherine started to panic and mopped up the coffee weaving its way between the keys and down the plughole of the inbuilt computer speakers. She started to look around to see if anyone else had witnessed her making a fool of herself in this café of cool. A young barista was calmly making his way from behind the counter with a cloth. Damn, had he seen the whole thing? She went into British mode, apologising for being alive before he could get a word in.

"*Desolée*. Sorry I seem to have made a bit of a mess of things."

He answered in American accented English "Looks as if you have. In more ways than one."

Catherine was still wiping away. She couldn't afford to lose the work in her computer and muttered to herself, "What a nightmare."

"No it's reality and the sooner you wake up and smell the coffee the better."

This comment had the effect of making Catherine look up from her hardware. Had he just said what he had said? Could he have been that forward? Yet he looked quite innocent, he couldn't have been more than twenty-five with that hipster look that made her feel like her own mother.

"Isn't that rather a personal marketing approach? And what would you know about it anyway?"

The barista seemed to take her rebuke in his stride, not losing his cool in any way. His mocca-dark eyes ground their way into hers.

"Hey ma'am, I'm in the coffee business. I know all there is to know about instant gratification, quick hits and morning after cures and if you ask me you're not in for a diluted Americano or the smooth milky ride of a cappuccino. Don't even think macchiato. Nothing can take the bitter edge off this one. We're talking espresso, ristretto. With no sugar."

Catherine had had her dose of sweet-talking, smart-talking and shit-spouting men for the day. She pushed her stuff into her on-trend sequined tote bag and stood up.

"Is there a good tea shop around here?"

Just as she was making her way out, the barista gave it another shot.

"Just leave everything to brew and let the leaves determine your future if you want to. I'd ground his beans and give him a good roasting myself."

***

Catherine was glad to pick up the children from a friend's house. She managed to ward off too many questions about her ashen features by using the "gastro" card. That was always the excuse to slap down when you wanted to avoid the endless pecks on the cheeks and make a quick getaway. After all, in France passing on the dreaded gastroenteritis was a deed tantamount to … well sleeping with your friend's husband. The only exception applied if your friend actually had a few kilos to lose, in which case she would practically beg you to French kiss her in the hope of a diet-free weight-loss solution. It wasn't exactly a detox spa retreat but equally effective and cheaper.

Back home the children had quickly picked up on the fact that there was a certain free-for-all going on and made the most of the chance to eat their way through the emergency shelf of the freezer and of the extended TV watching slots.

Their mother was avoiding any more direct human contact and back to finding answers by rubbing the genie of the Net. Maybe she could google her way through her situation. "Divorce lawyer" gave a spool of possibilities and she made a note of a few names. "Botox specialist" was inspired by her reflection in the mirror when she came home. The furrow between her eyes that she had always considered as a by-product of her writing, the burrowing of her brain for ideas, was starting to turn into a cavernous canyon of calamity.

Before getting down to writing that postponed mail to her editor, having disconnected skype to avoid further caffeine-fuelled disasters, she decided to see whether what was happening was written in the stars. Her daily horoscope read:

'Don't waste your time and effort crying over a spilt latte. Anyway are you sure that's what you ordered in the first place? Maybe your tastes have changed and you were just stuck in a routine that wasn't good for you. This may be a sign for you to start a new life ... so dry your eyes, clear up the mess and go for skinny, black or extra whipped cream. Just don't order the same old thing! You deserve better!'

Clearly already craving physical interaction, Catherine took her emotions out on the screen once again and started knocking on it.

"This is so weird. Oy, big brother. Can you actually see me?"

She started crying helplessly as she realised that what she really needed was a real live big brother. One who would just be there, protect her, give her a hug, tell her that she would get through it.

Being a single child, she had loved having a family of her own. Writing was a lonely business and the noise and hustle and bustle of being part of a bigger unit had balanced the monk-like existence to which her career choice had condemned her.

Was she putting the barriers of her cell back up by going it alone? Surely divorce was supposed to be a liberating experience. But what if she found herself alone with herself? She wasn't sure that she liked herself enough for that. But hey, as long as she had her children, she had all the freedom she needed.

CHAPTER 7

Separation is to divorce what purgatory is to hell, thought Catherine. It certainly felt as if she was sitting in the antechamber of Dante's *inferno* that morning. Failed marriages didn't seem to bring out the best in people to go by the angry couples and forlorn singles around her. The hate and resentment were tangible and could be heard above the hushed bickering and hurled abuse that, combined with the summer heatwave, were turning the divorce lawyer's waiting room into a pressure cooker.

Catherine took the only seat left next to a lady of a certain but undefinable age. She must have been quite a looker in her youth but had enough character in her face to age disgracefully. Her hair, piled sweepingly on top of her head was brash silver, her still startlingly blue eyes set in kohl and her mouth a crimson seal against the paper white of her skin. She sat there regally like an ageing Marie-Antoinette and seemingly oblivious to the screaming populace around her yet at the same time taking it all in.

She had been watching Catherine's every move, the incessant phone checking, the pushing back of the hair, the jolt each time one of the doors to the lawyers' offices opened.

"First time?" she asked in French in a voice thickly tiered with decades of experience and adventure.

Catherine was so taken aback at her grey self coming within the radar of such colourful extravagance that she wasn't sure how to respond.

"First appointment you mean?"

With a low laugh that brought to mind images of a cigarette holder held aloft by a gloved hand at Regine's nightclub in Paris, she corrected the younger woman's naivety.

"No, first divorce."

Feeling almost unworthy of the grand dame's worldliness, Catherine admitted it was the case.

"Don't worry. I'd been through a few already at your age."

Warming to this creature straight out of the Moulin Rouge, Catherine dared to ask "And now?"

She looked darkly at her but just when Catherine was starting to fear that she had overstepped the mark, the swirling mist that seemed to surround the bourgeoise lifted suddenly and she whispered back her answer confidentially.

"Let's say more than Sarkozy and fewer than Zsa Zsa Gabor. There must be something about the Hungarians."

"No, she was Polish... I mean…" but it was out before Catherine could stop herself.

The Bourgeoise patted her on the knee.

"Ah, Pole dancers, lap dancers, belly dancers, male ballet dancers. Do you know why Frenchmen are such infidels?"

"No why?"

"Simply because the French can can…" she whispered back with an endearing wink.

At that moment, a lawyer elegant enough to be worthy of such a client came striding down the hallway with open arms and greeted her like an old friend with an exuberant kiss on both cheeks.

"Mme de la Roche-Smith-Santos. Now have you remembered your loyalty card? You know the next one could be free!"

Mme de la Roche-Smith-Santos gave him a smile so charming as to explain away the multi-barrelled surname in one shot of Cupid's arrow.

"Oh my darling. The next time it will be the one. I am sure."

Putting her arm through the lawyer's, she turned back to look at Catherine.

"Never give up hope. The love of your life is always out there somewhere. You just need a good lawyer when it turns out that you have nine lives."

She leaned in closer and in a harder tone awash in the pungent notes of her perfume she added a word of warning.

"But remember, this is France, you don't need a lawyer who knows his stuff. You need a lawyer who knows the judge."

With a measured clicking of heels on the polished wood parquet flooring, she was gone, leaving Catherine sitting there in awe at this new world of apparent glamour and guts into which she was apparently entering. She felt a sudden urge to add shoulder pads to her jacket and gulp down a Bourbon from a crystal tumbler.

The actual appointment with the lawyer paled into a mundane formality after that. Far from the "we'll take him for everything he's got and leave the cheating swine wishing he'd never breached the Oder-Neisse line", it was more about share and share alike although she wasn't sure where like came into the equation.

After explaining the various options, divorce by mutual consent or for fault, but dissuading her from the latter because the jury was apparently out on its definition, the lawyer had promised to draw up the papers and saw her to the door, leaving her, once again, with the feeling that she'd just been had and that the men were all in this together.

Her back turned to the bronze plaque on the Haussmann-style building, Catherine paused to check her messages. Her heart lifted as she read and listened her way through the invitations from friends for coffee and wine and play dates with the children. One message in particular made her snap out of the surreal morning she had just spent. It was the bakery that she'd asked to make the cake for Arthur's birthday the following week. In the chaos of the last few days she'd forgotten to confirm.

Damn, that was another quandary to solve, one of the many stumbling blocks that lay ahead on this new path that she had been forced or chosen to tread, depending on perspective. Arthur was insisting on having his father at his party. No attempts at telling him that his father had rarely been at any of his jelly-guzzling jamborees had convinced him otherwise. He wanted his *maman* and his *papa* to be there. *Voila.*

Catherine suspected that Manon was the mastermind behind this plan, having seen a few too many Disney films consisting of children engineering reconciliations between unwitting and dim-witted parents. But she decided there and then that she would be strong enough by the party to cope with his presence. He could be a guest. She would just make sure he would be an unwelcome one.

CHAPTER 8

The week that followed, the first full week after signing up for the unknown, was a bit like booking a mystery hotel on a travel website. She had no idea where she was going.

Nothing had changed around her. The village with its golden stone walls still exuded its air of gentility. The market still came on the Wednesday to transform the car park overlooking the big city below into an open-air foodie paradise. The same faces could be seen chatting over a glass of Viognier at the bar, their bags of seasonal vegetables, herb-coated cured sausages and country bread propped up against their high stools.

The pizza van was still attracting its loyal customers, which meant that this Wednesday again, a good proportion of the village children would be lunching on a salmon and cream topped *Norvegienne* or a *Reine* with its scattering of ham and mushrooms.

The normality was unsettling given that, for Catherine, everything had changed. As she popped out to the market in her ubiquitous dark sunglasses, which she had even started wearing inside to hide her tears from the children, she suddenly felt out of place in this idyllic setting.

She was too imperfect, too much of a failure, too raw, too rough around the edges for this world of perfectly trimmed hedges, jeans with heels and shiny new cars.

After picking out her glossy red peppers and polished courgettes, smelling the melons and weighing them in her hand as if she'd been brought up in Provence rather than in a town perched on the cliffs above the Irish Sea, popping the punnets of local strawberries into her basket and swapping the usual banalities with the *primeur*, she let the children go off to the nearby playground for ten minutes while she took a seat on the café terrace and ordered a Perrier. The July sun was starting to send the locals to sit in the shade of the plane trees and into the air-conditioned coolness of the brasserie and the wine cellar's make-shift bar.

Catherine suddenly realised that women, all women, had taken on a strange fascination for her. She swiftly dismissed any emerging doubts that she'd been put off men for ever, but caught herself staring at the young waitress on duty. She was still in her early twenties, her skin youthfully taut and summer-tanned and her natural dark Southern European hair free of the desperate highlighting that turned older women into the slaves of their roots and the cash cows of their hairdressers.

The girl was joking easily with all the male customers, not flirting but clearly at ease in their company. Catherine could imagine her attraction, her uncomplicated juvenility, her care-free abandon.

How could she compete?

She looked on enviously as a mother with a toddler walked past, the little boy shrieking with delight as his *maman* lifted him off his feet in play. She longed for the innocence of those early days, for that smug feeling of having created a family unit, when nothing can deflect your certainty that you will have a perfect life, even when the cracks are already staring you in the face. The young woman was pretty, trendily dressed and was clearly revelling in the time she was spending with her son. The vomit factor increased further when she reached the end of the road only to be greeted with a long kiss by a good looking young man who hauled the toddler up onto his shoulders.

Despite her envy, Catherine only hoped that they would go the distance. That they would continue to skip through their lives hand in hand.

Two middle-aged women came to sit at a table in front of her. She caught herself. Middle-aged? They were probably only slightly older than her. They were of the well-conserved variety, clearly not worn by work or financial constraints, expensively dressed and weighed down by the accoutrements of their designer handbags and conspicuous jewellery.

Catherine searched their faces for the tell-tale signs of betrayal and resignation. Were they being paid to stay? Were their luxury city runabouts the price the husbands had to fork out for their silence? A mini price for a maximum of freedom? Did they also have toy boys to run around with in their toy cars? Was that where she was going wrong. Was that what she was supposed to do, accept that, after fifteen years, monogamy had been thrown out with the baby's bath water and that soon-to-be teen-aged children meant a second adolescence also for the parents?

Then it struck Catherine that the women's faces were as line free as that of the waitress. She thought back to her laughter lines forged by the good times and her frown lines excavated by the bad times that were starting to torment her. Were these ladies' lives so lacking in highs and lows as to make their faces a permanent level ground?

She clearly had some filling work to catch up on. She got out her phone and called the number of the Botox clinic she had found on the internet the other day. It was bad enough being scarred for life on the inside, she would just give it a try to see if you could artificially smooth out the stigmata of her separation. Just the once. Just to make her feel human again if that was possible with humanoid features.

Leaving the money for her water on the table, she picked up her basket and fetched the children from the swings and roundabouts and walked back to the house with them, chatting about those instant playmates they had just made in the park. A child's version of the one-night stand, they were fun but not to be mistaken for real friendships that were cultivated over years and, if lucky, lasted into adulthood and forever and ever, cross your fingers hope to die.

It was easy when sex and mortgages didn't come into play.

She paused before opening the gate to take out the post. In the age of the internet there seemed to be fewer and fewer letters but an increasing number of catalogues. Wedged in between the sales blurb of the local optician and the latest hypermarket offers was a discreet white envelope with a local postmark. The absence of lettering spoke volumes.

She picked it up with trepidation and held it tightly in her hand as she opened the door in the hedge that led into their garden, hauled her shopping basket down the garden path, unlocked the front door and went into the relative coolness of the house.

She sent the children off to wash their hands before lunch, which they did begrudgingly as if being punished for playing outside. As soon as she was alone she dumped her groceries on the island in the kitchen and went out to the shady terrace to be alone.

Her legs were starting to tremble. She knew it was the result of the blood test. How careful had her husband been? In his choice of mistress or mistresses and in his behaviour? Responsible wasn't exactly his middle name. His flamboyancy had been part of the initial attraction but there was a limit on just how much you wanted to flaunt it.

HIV, Hepatitis, Gonorrhoea, Syphilis. They sounded like the names of a rock star's offspring. She may have been level-headed enough to get the tests done as soon as possible but now the thought that she would have to deal with the consequences was doing her head in. God how she hated him for putting her in this situation.

Her hands now imitating the tremors in her legs, she ripped open the envelope, tearing the paper. All she could see before her eyes were lists of letters and figures, the science clouding the facts. None of it made any sense to her. When they put negative was that positive? Or was it the positive that was negative? Why didn't they make it easier? Put a thumbs up or thumbs down sign like a scuba diver to say that she could come up for air or descend into the murkiness below.

She took a deep breath to blow away the clouds gathering in her brain and went through it all methodically, line by line.

After a few minutes of careful examination and adding the pluses and minuses, she gave a sigh of relief. It was positive. She was negative. On all counts.

At least he'd been playing a clean game.

Relieved it was one less thing she had to deal with, but still unable to stand up she threw herself back on the cushions and started to cry. Again. Uncontrollably.

CHAPTER 9

Florence could hear the untidy sobbing seep through the artfully arranged cypress trees and lavender bushes in her Provence-inspired landscaped garden. That's all she needed. It was bad enough not being in St Tropez this week with their group of best friends. The couple who owned the holiday home had announced only the previous week that they were separating, pouring ice cold rosé over all their plans by cancelling the group holiday at the last minute.

Bloody divorce. Really, people didn't think about the consequences for her social life. Dinner parties with single white female forty-somethings flirting with the husbands and getting all teary after the second glass of Côte Rôtie spoilt the fun for everyone and, on top of that, was a waste of good wine. 'Let them drink Châsse Spleen', as Marie-Antoinette would surely have said.

She was trying to get to grips with yet another historical biography about that very woman of substance when the asthmatic heaving again dragged her out of the Petit Trianon in Versailles where the Austrian queen was still partying like it was before 1789.

Florence sighed. She guessed it was Catherine, the *Galloise* who lived next door, as all the other neighbours seemed to be away, the *veinards*, the lucky buggers. She'd heard on the grapevine that she'd lost her father the other day. She was probably having a bit of a cry about that. The Welsh obviously didn't have the same discretion as the phlegmatic English.

The uninhibited howling was threatening to trigger a tsunami in her swimming pool. Mon dieu, it was like having a dramatic Italian living next door. Especially in the last few weeks when she and her husband had suddenly started to take their arguments *al fresco.*

She put her book down next to the pre-lunch cocktail on the low table next to the lounger, stood up, wrapped the sarong brought back from Mauritius last Christmas around her caffeine, nicotine and beauty routine-honed body, fetched the keys from the kitchen and grudgingly flip flopped down the drive before Catherine breached the sacrosanct lunchtime noise ban by setting off the pool alarm after throwing herself into a chlorinated grave.

The banshee wailing got louder as she neared the Dupont gate. She sighed again but, thinking about the Catholic good deed points she was clocking up, not to mention the potential gossip rewards, she rang the doorbell.

The crying stopped like a Baby Tears turned back the right way around. Then there was silence. But *merde*, now she was there and she didn't want it to be a wasted journey so stubbornly Florence pressed the bell again, for longer this time.

After a few long seconds, she heard the intercom come to life inside the house and a voice muffled by wires and probably a thick mix of saline mucus.

"*Oui?*"

"Yes Catherine, *c'est moi*, Florence, your *voisine*," she said in her best English. "Is everything ok? Are you ok? Are the children ok?"

There was no answer and she was starting to think that her neighbour had hung up on her. Her beautifully manicured finger was about to stab the button again when the buzz of the door made her leap back in surprise. She pushed it open before it auto-locked itself again and, after years of distant neighbourly cordiality, walked into the life and loves of the Duponts.

As Florence walked down the path towards the house she could make out Catherine, or at least what was left of her, cowering in the half-open doorway. What did they say in English? She was no oil painting, unless you compared her with that crazed, gaunt and ashen guy from Munch's 'The Scream'.

As the door opened wider to let her in, she took in the magma-rimmed eyes set in volcanic pits and the trails left by the molten lava of her tears along the ridges of her neighbour's craggy features.

Something inside her told her that this wasn't just about her father's death. Sensing that Catherine couldn't bring herself to talk, the lips trembling with the effort of keeping face, or at least keeping her face together, Florence exercised the prerogative of her ten year seniority and took matters into her own hands, leading her back into the lounge and sitting her down on the most comfortable armchair.

"Catherine, Catherine. What's wrong? With your crying you're turning this into the wettest summer on record. *Qu'est ce qui se passe?*"

Catherine looked over at her neighbour, perched on the sofa opposite her in her bright sarong, sunglasses keeping back her thick dark, shoulder-length hair, her Hermes keyring holder clasped in her work-spared hands.

It was strange seeing her in the house in such casual attire. They were on friendly terms. With Jacques she had been a frequent guest at her numerous aperitifs or summer parties and Catherine would be invited along to the daytime sales parties she organised for exquisite Belgian designer homeware or bourgeois-bohemian jewellery and they would chat on the street outside. But this impromptu visit was like having the queen in unannounced for elevenses when she was out of digestives to dunk in their coffees.

Florence could see the *Galloise* scour her head for an answer, could see the panic in her eyes as she considered whether to tell the truth or dare a lie. She decided to prompt her.

"Is it something to do with Jacques?"

In her experience, after death, the only other human tragedy that could cause such pain were men.

She'd obviously hit the right button, as the tears spurted once again from Catherine's eyes, but silently this time. Thinking about all her lost sun-time, she decided to spur the revelations on a bit with another prompt.

"Tell me what it is that he has done to you?"

The compassion-veiled curiosity opened the floodgates. Feeling the release and the relief, for the first time since that Facebook teaser, Catherine told someone what she had discovered on that fateful night just over a week ago, the longest week in her life. The other woman. The mistress. The years of infidelity. The double life. The fact that they worked together. Her weekends alone with the children. His weekend breaks with the other woman. Her father. His death. Jacques practically cheating on her on the freshly dug earth of the grave. The lies. The treason. The eviction. The end.

Florence listened. But while her face and body were miming the shock, horror and disgust that Catherine needed to see, inside, she just felt a Groundhog Day fatigue. It was always the same story, admittedly with a few geographical changes or fetishist tweaks, but, at the end of the day, this was only yet another believer having to contend with the inexistence of the happy ever after.

It was worse for the foreign ones she found, the kind, happy-go-lucky ones who found themselves in the country that had invented the phrase "*trop bonne, trop conne*". They were too much of a soft touch, they were the ones who were hit the hardest.

Florence had been there herself, who hadn't? But she wasn't going to dish out any advice. The poor thing didn't need the truth and didn't need the lies. What she needed was a way to cope with it. And so Florence did what one of her friends had done to her when she had found the passenger seat in her husband's car in the recline position and a stiletto heel mark dug into the car mat. She opened the key holder and took out the thin panacea, the legal high for those down in the dumps.

Catherine stared at the six capsules, trying to work out how that was the solution. Were they a magic potion that would erase the past and let her go back to a time and place where all of this hadn't yet happened? Or was she supposed to slip the six droughts into her husband's water-clouded Pernod to seek the ultimate revenge?

She looked up at Florence questioningly, who answered in her usual mix of adult French and childhood English.

"It is like Alice, *ma chérie*," they will take you into wonderland until you come out of this *merde.*"

CHAPTER 10

Right, she could do this. Four days to go before the party, and she had her secret weapon. That super power invisible to everyone else made her even stronger. It was inside her.

Her first day on an anti-depressant drug had been and gone. Catherine had looked at the blue and white mini torpedoes in their aluminium casing for at least an hour after Florence had left and as the children spent their siesta in the TV room, hooked to the constant supply from the wall-mounted dealer of escapism.

She had then popped them into her mouth and waited for something to happen. What she had expected, she didn't know. A kind of psychedelic experience where she felt only love for all mankind despite the fact that most of their kind seemed to train their weapons on anything that moved? Or at least a Eureka moment that would tell her exactly what was her best solution for the future?

To be honest, it had been no more effective than a cup of tea and a digestive and she had gone to flop down among the cushions and the children, which had given her a much stronger sense of well-being and was much more addictive.

Now on her second day on drugs she was preparing everyone to get ready to go shopping for the party. The second pill was sending out its active substances to patrol her body, ready to take on any depressing thought and slay it before it could bring her down.

She could feel the agitation, could hear her voice suddenly cranking up a notch like a choirboy whose voice is starting to break.

She had so many things to do and not enough time to do it, my god Florence was right, it was like stepping into Wonderland, except that she wasn't Alice, as she muttered to herself.

"Oh dear! Oh dear! I shall be too late," she felt more like the bloody rabbit!

By the time the two children were in the car, that she had gone back to the house three times, the first time to fetch the reusable shopping bags, the second time to fetch her handbag, and the third to fetch the party shopping list from the kitchen counter, she could feel the pearls of sweat bobsleighing down her limbs.

As she turned the car into the empty main road, the inside of her head felt like a scroll-down menu of to-do lists rolling up and down in an over-heated computer. The midday sun made the lines of the curb and flower beds melt like Dali watches, the heat contorting them into undulating shapes as she drove past.

Something felt strange, as if the whole world was caving in on her. And then things started to go seriously wrong. Even the car coming towards her seemed to be on a head-on collision course with her and was starting to swerve just like the rest of the surroundings. What was going on? Then as she saw the daytime flashing of lights and horn-sounding she suddenly realised why. She was on the wrong side of the road. She was driving on the left in a country where the right side was the right side to drive.

At the last minute, she swerved back into the right lane, just missing the fist-raised, swear-mouthed driver she'd just scared the wits out of in the Renault Clio.

Her hands were convulsed in cold turkey-like jitters on the steering wheel and her heart was beating with the speed of a rock band drummer as she continued on her way to the supermarket, looking over the shoulders every few minutes in case the gendarmes were on her heels to catch up with the crazy Brit who didn't know the French highway code.

She'd been in France for too long to make such a beginner's mistake. She was usually in automatic French driving mode. What was that atavistic pull that had drawn her to the left side of the road? Or was it just the pills taking away all her powers of rational thought?

When they reached the hypermarket, Catherine took the children for a cold drink to cool their nerves and downed a double espresso to bolster hers. But as she raced her way around the aisles, she felt the caffeine fix join forces with the white powder being sniffed up by her cells. Euphorically, she threw the party plates, streamer sprays and sugar-saturated drinks and sweets into the trolley, promising Arthur the bash of a lifetime.

By the time she was back in the car after returning the trolley to its nesting place by wheeling it back with an adolescent joy-ride abandon, Catherine felt like a manic optimist. Worse, she felt as if she was raring to go in every sense. She was even starting to feel from the waist down, an area which up until only yesterday had been firmly immobilised by the iron clinch of an imaginary chastity belt.

She felt better, much better.

"Let's listen to some music," she told the bemused and slightly concerned children and after floundering around in the glove compartment for a few minutes, popped a CD into the player and started the car.

Flirtatiously thanking the driver who patiently waited for her to reverse back from her parking space, she drew out and, singing along raucously to the music, she pushed the gear back into first and drove off with screeching tyres … right into the concrete bollard that had come out of nowhere to rather unkindly remind her that there were still obstacles in her path.

Bonnie Tyler was still "Lost in France" as the car was towed away and Catherine and the children piled the shopping into the boot of the waiting taxi.

As soon as she got home, Catherine buried the anti-depressants at the back of the medicine cupboard, shelving at the same time her hope of an easy-way-out. Back in the kitchen she made herself a nice cup of tea and decided that she would just have to take all the *"merde"*, as Florence called it, as it came, without artificial sweeteners.

CHAPTER 11

Did the guy who invented the nerf gun have a bad relationship with his mother, Catherine was thinking as yet another eight-year old boy took aim at her and at various objects around her home. They were certainly designed to get on your *nerfs* and she was starting to harbour nostalgic feelings about her two-day anti-depressant habit.

Arthur's party was in full swing, a couple of Tarzans doing just that from the trees in the garden and others taking one at the piñata hanging from another tree with a Star Wars lightsabre. Before they managed to break it apart and spoil the fun for everyone else Catherine herded everyone into the living room for one of the party games she had optimistically laid on, hoping to get away with one last traditional birthday party before she had to spend the next few years in Laserama's plastic-coated waiting room full of coke-doped adolescents.

True to his word for once, Jacques actually turned up. She let him into the house without a word and left it to the children to do all of the greeting. He looked up at her over their hugs. It was the first time he'd seen her since the Skype coffee debacle.

She turned her face away as she felt him staring at her.

"You look different," he said.

He continued to look her up and down, searching for the difference, as if he hadn't focused on her properly in years. The fact that he failed to notice the 6 kilos she had cried off and the acid-induced smoothness of her forehead spoke volumes about the attention he'd paid her in the past few years. Catherine turned away as the doorbell rang to announce that the show was on, not wanting him to see what was only an invisible plaster on the wound he had inflicted.

Jacques welcomed the guests and their parents with a performance that could have earned him a trip up the red-carpeted steps in Cannes. But then if you could glamorise toilet paper, you could pimp up a failed marriage. When he tried to put his arm around her waist as he was waving off a charmed mother and promising to keep her son away from peanuts or any other nut, it had taken all of Catherine's non-Latin stiff-upper-lip not to give him a thick one.

As she sat there with the children trying to explain the basic principles of pass the parcel to the non-English ones, not bred on party games that required certain rules to be obeyed, the fact that they had to wait for the music to stop before they could rip off the layers of paper and that no, they couldn't hold onto the parcel until the music stopped, Jacques plumped himself down beside her. She pressed the button on her phone to start the music and was getting ready to umpire when she heard,

"I got your divorce papers today."

"I got yours as well. First time anything's come together since we got married," she retorted.

The parcel and snide comments went around and around, layers of paper and unspoken truths being ripped off each time leaving a big pile of waste and destruction at the heart of the circle.

The next game up on the party menu was musical chairs. Another parody of marriage thought Catherine. You think you're safely ensconced on your seat and are suddenly dislodged as soon as your back is turned. She shared the thought with Jacques when he took the seat vacant next to her.

"Yes well it takes two to Tango. And that reminds me, the judge may like to hear about a certain Argentine guy …"

Catherine hissed back at him while keeping up her perfect hostess smile for the sake of the children.

"How dare you bring up the Argentine. That was fifteen years ago. We weren't even married. It was liquor not love, a double gin and tonic and a *paso doble* not a double life!"

"I'm just saying … who knows what you've been up to …."

With that he snatched the chair she was about to sit on and laughed as Catherine ended up in a rather inelegant posture on the floor. The children joined in the laughter thinking that Arthur's parents were great sports to be so willing to make fools of themselves like this.

Catherine got back up, brushing off the bits of balloon and streamers that were starting to make her house look like the ground cover of a psychedelic autumn forest and tried to get the kids to sit down for the next game.

She had invented her own pin-the-tail-on-the-donkey to make it more relevant for the international hotchpotch of party guests. Instead of an ass, which would have been more relevant to her, the eye-bound player had to blindly approach a map of Europe and pin the French flag as close to France as possible.

Jacques started encouraging the innocent little Lucas, who was Napoleonic in his insistence that the French Empire's borders were much further to the East than actually the case. He tried to pin down

Catherine's gaze as he taunted her with his instructions to poor old Lucas as he hovered over Berlin like a Luftbrücke pilot.

"A bit to the right Lucas, you're getting hotter."

The poor boy ended up with the French flag firmly planted in Krakow and a booby prize.

This was the last straw for Catherine who made the most of the pool-side "Simon says" session to give him his ultimatum.

"Right, I've had enough. I can't bear your presence. Just go away, back to wherever you're living or whoever you're staying with at the moment."

He started to tell her that she couldn't tell him what to do but only the plastic ducks head down in the swimming pool actually heard the words "This is still my house" that floated up to the surface in speech bubbles.

"Catherine says bye bye," she said as he spluttered his way up the ladder to roars of laughter from the children who were thrilled by the funny show put on by this amazing mum and dad duo and who would be asking their own progenitors for the same display at their next birthday.

Jacques had no choice but to make a soaked exit, his clothes having been executed, extinguished or exported by his vengeful wife. He turned back to her at the gate she was holding open for him in victory.

"I'll be picking the children up tomorrow to take them on holiday. I hope it will give you time to reflect on the decision before you destroy their lives forever."

"Or maybe it's the perfect moment to tell them that Father Christmas doesn't exist and that the tooth fairy is a gay dentist. What's one more delusion?"

With that she burst the balloons decorating the entrance and headed back to the party.

CHAPTER 12

The dream house, the ideal family home, seemed to be out in empathy with her. She hadn't had the energy or the will-power to clean up after Arthur's party the day before and it seemed to be haunted by ghostly traces of impish hands on usually gleaming French window glass, garish cobwebs of silly string across salvaged and lovingly restored Louis something-or-other furniture, the eerie crunch of popcorn on parquet flooring and the moans of the hung and quartered piñata still dancing out its death throes to the rhythm of the wind outside.

Catherine was only a shadow of her former self as she wandered lethargically around the house. The children had left with their father that morning with a caseful of lies, happy to go down to the coast but, she imagined, with that sinking feeling deep in their stomach that they had left something behind. When would it start to hit them that it was her?

She opened the fridge. Closed the fridge. She opened the drinks cabinet. Closed the drinks cabinet. She sat at the piano, raised the cover and played one of the few pieces she knew by heart. It was too cheerful for the occasion. She brought her fist down on the keyboard and then her forehead. The jarring notes were more fitting.

She floated aimlessly into the TV room with its comfy old sofas and big screen. She switched on the TV. She zapped between the rocambolesque French films from the 1960s so bad as to be cult, the 24-hour news channels that manage to find only four pieces of broadcast-worthy pieces of information and then go on to repeat them every five minutes for the entire day and the American series dubbed into direness without seeing anything she had any remote interest in watching. She opened her laptop but slammed it down even before it had booted fully, annoyed by the fact that even it seemed have joined the slow life movement.

She went back to the kitchen, half-heartedly throwing dirty paper plates into black plastic bags and starting to feel the emptiness sweeping in to replace each reminder of children's laughter bagged and binned. She was missing them so much and they had only been gone a few hours. They would soon be arriving at the beach house.

The anger swelled inside her at the thought that he had the immense privilege of being with the children. Should she have gone with them? Impossible. There was no way that she could have kept up the act in front of them. One afternoon with Jacques the previous day had showed her that she was not ready to forgive and forget. The blinkers were off. She was starting to see another side to him that he had either kept from her over the years or that she had chosen to ignore.

Had she just been chasing the French dream? Had she married the idea of a love that bridged seas and backgrounds and language barriers, not realising that after scaling the lofty heights, landfall is inevitable at one point.

She hadn't made it to the other shore. She was in the middle of that bridge that she had chosen to cross but was now standing on the parapet waiting to jump. She couldn't go back because that meant going home. That meant failure. That meant she had been wrong. And she couldn't carry on because the pillars holding the bridge couldn't be relied on. They could crumble at any time. No, jumping was definitely the better option. It was a long drop but with no going back or forwards what else could she do?

She realised that she was standing there spooning Nutella into her mouth. As she stood staring at the local ambrosia, a thought came to her and she gave a chocolate-toothed smile.

"Let's hit him where it really hurts."

***

As was the family tradition, Jacques and the children were already hitting the waves before even unloading the car. They kicked off their shoes and left their clothes on the sand to enjoy that first delectable feeling of the sea on their skin. The children paid no heed to their father when he had had enough and tried to convince them that it was only the first dip of many. So while they continued to jump over the waves and scream in delight as their force tackled them into the foam, Jacques sat on the shoreline.

That's when it struck him that it was just them and him for the week. No more sleeping in while Catherine got the still-steaming baguettes from the local *boulangerie* for the children's breakfast, no refreshing salads miraculously served up at lunchtime after a few glasses of the local aperitif, no restorative siestas while Catherine kept the children stimulated and busy when it was too hot to go outside. No one to babysit while he popped out to the local bar to catch up on the latest sports results.

Instinctively he started looking around as if help could be mustered up somehow by feigning to be lost and in need of tender loving care. Weren't single dads with children the way to a woman's heart? But somehow all the women who were browning their June-starved bodies around him only seemed to give him withering looks as soon as they saw him staring. It was going to be a long week.

He finally got the children back to the beach house with promises of a lunch of doughnuts and coke bought from the nomadic vendor endlessly trudging along the sand looking for a fertile oasis of custom.

Jacques saw that Catherine was Skyping them and passed his phone to his daughter whose face lit up with hope.

"Hi *maman*, I miss you."

"I know darling. I miss you too. And your brother. But it's just a week and we'll Skype every day ok?"

Arthur's heart-melting little face came into the frame.

"Do you really have to work mum? Can't you come on holiday with us?"

"I wish I could darling but you'll be going with me on holiday to Wales to see Grandma soon. *Papa* is there to look after you. I need to work. I have a lot of things to work out …"

But Arthur was already visible only in profile having spotted a group of boys playing football on the beach.

"I can see one of the friends I made last year *maman. Bisous. Bisous.*" And he was off.

After exchanging virtual love, kisses and hugs with Manon, her daughter gave the phone back to her father and Catherine was forced to look into his dark eyes that reflected only a darker soul.

"Satisfied now? What it's like being responsible for the first time in your life?"

Nothing could have prepared her for the response as he poured the briny Mediterranean water onto her still gaping wound.

"If I can't cope, I can always call Maria. She'll be there for me. She won't leave me. She won't throw me out. She'll love me … and the children, even if you won't."

Something broke inside her.

"You bastard. She will not get within a mile of my children do you hear me! But hey when you know you can be replaced by a hooker and a cleaner then you know there's nothing much to save in a marriage. She can have you. Those kinds of girls can be bought from a catalogue. They're one a penny. I can't be bought. I have to be earned. But you don't deserve my love. I'm logging off. Forever. Definitively. I've been living with a ghost for 18 years so maybe I'll just turn into one as well. I'm dead to you anyway and have been for years …"

"Catherine, don't be stupid…"

***

Taking a mistress was one thing. Taking on another mother for their children after only a few weeks of separation was another thing completely. She couldn't breathe as she imagined the woman whose hands had roamed all over her husband's body tying back her daughter's hair or wiping her son's face.

The reality of divorce once again hit home. But if home is where the heart is then Jacques definitely wasn't her des res. Home was wherever her children were. And she couldn't let a burglar in who would take them away from her.

This was just too difficult for her. She wasn't made for such high drama. And it was clearly just the beginning. Her father had just died, her husband was dead to her and now he was threatening to sever her from her life blood. Crazed, she decided to get there first to deprive him of the satisfaction.

Getting up from her prostrate position and pushing back up the toilet seat that had slowly come down in sympathy or shame over her head, she started rummaging in the bathroom cupboards. Where were the razors when you needed them? All she could find were wax and depilatory cream. What was she supposed to do? Boil herself to death in hot wax? Eat a tube of Nair and dissolve herself from the inside. All they'd find would be a blob of hair-incrusted cream on the floor. Hair today, gone tomorrow.

Resuming her search for life relief she took out the anti-depressants that Florence had pushed on her only a week ago. After that unfortunate first experience, they had been immediately ditched and dumped in the back of the first aid box, forced to draw on their own active substances to overcome their woe over their own fate. Catherine looked down at them.

"If I take too many of these, will I just laugh myself to death?"

Looking down at the driveway from the bathroom window she saw her eco-friendly, conscience-boosting hybrid car, fresh back from the garage after its car park bumper car experience. "And can you actually gas yourself to death in an electric car?"

Foiled in her attempts at suicide in the bathroom she went back to the kitchen and took out the bleach from under the sink. She unscrewed the top and her last thought was that at least her mum would be glad that she'd "made a clean job of it for once". Clearing up cups of coffee after her from every conceivable and inconceivable surface in the house had been her mum's contribution to her writing career. However, she sensed that her literary achievements had never made her mother proud in the way that seeing her daughter crowned housekeeper of the year would have made her.

Just as she was about to turn herself into a Domestos Goddess, Catherine's crazed gaze landed on the selfie of her and the children stuck to the fridge door. They needed her. She couldn't abandon them. They needed her to be strong. They needed her to be alive. They needed her to be amazing.

Throwing the bleach down the kitchen sink where it would do more good than harm, she strode resolutely to the bedroom, put on the kind of music that had you winning boxing tournaments when you're past your prime, stripped down to her bra and knickers and jumped onto the Nordic Walker.

An hour later she was still determined to end her marriage and bugger the vows. She would divide and conquer and not hold on desperately "'til death do us part".

CHAPTER 13

One of her biggest sacrifices in her years as loyal *épouse* and devoted mother had been the cinema. Catherine loved everything about going to the cinema, from picking out the film to the sickly sweet smell of popcorn. There were things she missed in these days of the big cinema complexes, the demise of the dramatic curtains that would glide open to reveal the screen in her old cinema back home and the corny adverts for local carpet showrooms with seventies-haired women stroking similarly coiffed golden retrievers on orange-coloured mats, but once the room darkened, you could sit back and enjoy sharing a moment of escapism with a room of other people.

Escapism was just what she was in need of now and was on her way towards it. She was even feeling happy were it not for the incessant ringing of her phone all the way to the big screen complex on the city outskirts. Jacques Dupont's name came up as the single credit on the display of the on-board computer, but that was one summer release she hadn't enjoyed at all.

As soon as she got to the underground carpark she switched off her phone to keep out the reality and get ready to step into other people's lives.

She hadn't checked the screening times before she left the house on a whim and had an hour to kill before the film she wanted to see was showing. She picked up the free cinema magazine to see what other films could fill in the week ahead for her and boost her cinema attendance average for the year and took a seat at the bar.

She ordered a beer and sat there for a while. Her speed reading skills were proving to be a disadvantage though and she had already worked her way through the articles after ten minutes. Fight as hard as she might the day's events were coming back to her. As dusk fell outside her thoughts also darkened as she suddenly remembered how depressing it was to go to the cinema on your own.

Around her she could spot the young couples on their first dates, waiting only for the lights to be cut in the auditorium so that they could get up close and personal, the married couples cuddling up in guilty ecstasy at having an evening away from the kids and the bunch of friends revving themselves up for the latest Hollywood blockbuster.

She was lost in dejection when she realised that man was standing in front of her, three children in tow. He seemed to be trying to catch her eye.

"Bonsoir."

Catherine automatically returned the greeting but with a hint of a query in hers.

"I don't want to disturb you but I've seen you at school. You're Manon's mum aren't you?"

"Erm... yes."

"I just wanted to check you were ok. You looked a bit, well, distant…."

Catherine felt herself reddening and blushing like a Geisha on her first outing, but somehow failed to muster up the same discretion.

"Yes, no, yes I'm fine. Sorry, I mean, my mind was ... I'm fine, it's just well, it's just my first week without the children."

She kicked herself for coming out with such an idiotic answer. She would never get that continental blasé coolness right. She needed to take up smoking and wearing black Zadig et Voltaire.

'School dad' seemed to be taking it all in his stride though and gave her a warm smile.

"Ah I think I know what you mean. If it helps in any way I went through the same thing recently. Break-ups are never easy. Are you sure you're ok?"

"Yes, yes fine. Just not a great day. Not a great week. Not a great summer."

He gave her another smile but she could read the scepticism in his eyes and took leave of her with the children.

"See you at school pick up next term maybe."

Catherine smiled bravely at the four as they turned away to go to their film thinking that "school pick up" was the only picking up that was likely to play any role in her life for the next few years and gulped down the remainder of her beer to drown out the raising angst in her stomach.

She couldn't sit still and went to stand outside the theatre even if the previous film was still reaching its final earth-shattering climax behind the doors. 'School dad', as she had come to think of him given that she had no idea what his name was, was doing the same beside the next door down, playing around with his 3D glasses to amuse his offspring as they waited. He did a mean Stevie Wonder.

When he noticed her looking he took them off without a hint of embarrassment and with a word to the children walked over to her.

"So what are you going to see? Nothing depressing I hope."

He looked up at the electronic sign above the door.

"'Melancholia'? I'm not sure it's what you need at the moment."

"Yes well somehow I didn't feel like a romantic comedy."

He smiled.

"You're right. Look, don't take this the wrong way but this is my number. I'm in town this week. Everyone else seems to be away. You know us French, we don't like to work in the summer. It's August so we close the office! I don't like to think of you on your own. Just call me if you need anything. No obligation. Ok?"

Catherine once again proved to herself that eighteen years without dating or flirting had taken their toll.

"Yes I know, it's that week, when everyone is away on holiday. Except us sad cases. If I really hit rock bottom I'll call you."

Catherine registered his bemused smile and tried to dig her way out of the grave of singledom she was busy digging for herself.

"Oh God, I didn't mean it that way. It's nothing against you…"

But 'school dad' was laughing outright by now.

"Don't worry I know what you mean. If I'm the last man left on earth … Just think of me as your fairy godmother."

With that he took flight back to his kids who were warning him that the film was about to start. As they went in his oldest son commented on the scene.

"I've seen her on the school car park but she's usually very smiley. The kind of mum who's doesn't treat you like a nothing just because you don't go to pony club with her *petit chéri*."

His daughter chipped in.

"*Oui*, she's always turning up looking cheerful in green Wellington boots and old jeans but still looks better than some of the other mums in their designer stuff."

"Yes", said school dad, "she seems like a very *charmante femme*. She just needs someone to put the smile back on that pretty face of hers."

***

Two hours later Catherine was caught up in the flow of lay critics streaming out of the cinema. The subject matter may not have been a laugh a minute but she was just happy to be doing something normal, to be part of a crowd, not caught up in her own troubles. She reached into her jeans pocket to take out the telephone number school dad had given her. The name Romain was scribbled on the piece of paper. He had a name. She doubted that she'd phone though. But just having the number gave her comfort and hope and she put it back safely into her pocket, confident that things could only get better.

CHAPTER 14

The burst of hope was short-lived. Things weren't getting better. They were getting worse.

Shattered glass was making a perilous skating rink of her kitchen floor. All she could do was stare at it, petrified. The kitchen window and shutters were closed but not locked. Did that mean that the burglars had come and gone, but why carefully shut them behind them? Or did it mean that they were still in the house, lurking somewhere as they got ready to attack her?

She went back into the hall and with her back to the front door, ready to escape if needed, delved into the murky depths of her handbag to find her phone among the lipsticks, pens, scrolls of hypermarket receipts, loyalty cards from restaurants she'd eaten in once abroad and wasn't likely to return to and one odd child's sock that seemed to have adopted permanent residence in there along with her purse and car keys. She hadn't looked at her phone since going into the cinema and it took her what seemed like hours to switch it on again, type in the code and wait for the network connection.

That's when she saw them, the tens of missed calls. What was going on? Not hearing any noise of any intruder in the house she decided to first of all listen to her messages. It could give her a clue to what was going on.

Her messages started with one from Jacques, the ones she had purposely ignored when she jumped into the car earlier that evening.

They increased in intensity and told her the entire story of what had been going on in a series of telephonic chapters.

"Just answer the phone Catherine. I need to know you're ok."

He should have thought of that sooner she thought. Delete.

"Come on, don't be *stupide*. Think of the kids. Even if you hate me. Even if we are over, I'm sure there is some future for you."

So kind of him. Delete.

"Don't kill yourself over me. Please. I couldn't live with it. What will people think?"

The sheer arrogance of the man, he was driving the nails into his own coffin, not hers. Delete

"Ok that's it. If you don't answer in the next five minutes, I'm phoning the police."

What the hell was he up to? Did he really think that he was worth killing herself over? Ok it may have crossed her mind for a fleeting second but why would she give him the satisfaction?

Another message was still hiding among the red digits admonishing her for her absence. She didn't recognise the number and listened.

"*Bonsoir madame*, I am Commandant Varenne of the Gendarmerie of St Desirée. We are in your home at present after the alert was given by your husband. We are trying to locate you. Please call us as soon as you get this message. We need to know where you are and ascertain that you are safe. Call me back on this number. *Merci*."

Catherine dialled her husband's number, livid with anger. Was he trying to pass her off as crazy? As a danger to herself? He had no time to finish his *allo*…

"What the hell have you done? I was at the cinema for god's sake! Why should I kill myself? You're the one who should be shot … but hey I'm sure it was just wishful thinking …"

Her rant was interrupted by the ringing of the doorbell. She hung up without another word and angrily opened the door, the violation of the house exacerbated by this violation of her privacy.

Two uniformed gendarmes were standing there and seemed surprised to see her. They took in her hair, a frenzied mass where her hands had passed through it in frustration and the thin slits of her draconian eyes sending fiery beams in their direction.

"So you are home. You know that you have scared a lot of people tonight?"

Catherine was flabbergasted.

"I don't understand. Since when has going to the cinema been a crime? I switched the phone off like a good citizen. That's what you're supposed to do isn't it?"

The gendarme who was doing all the talking continued, indicating at the same time to the other one that he should go in and take a look.

"Yes but you led your husband to believe that you were going to create some drama of your own *n'est-ce pas*?"

"That's nonsense. I may just have mentioned something about the death of our marriage…"

"But you forget *madame* that we have seen the state of the house. All the signs are there."

"What signs?"

At that point, the second gendarme who had just stood there in his breeches and little cap until then, nudged the gendarme who had been trying to get some kind of confession of suicidal tendencies out of her. It was all completely surreal, as if the cinema was gradually seeping itself into her life.

The second gendarme pointed to the bottle of bleach on the kitchen counter. Catherine saw the gesture and rolled her eyes.

"It's not what you think. I was bleaching the house, not my stomach, cleaning my husband's contamination away…"

He picked up the almost empty bottle of vodka and raised his eyebrow in interrogation.

"Just a bit of Eastern Comfort. My husband's favourite tipple."

He clearly thought she was off her head. You clearly couldn't trust anyone who put mint sauce on lamb. "I am not reassured *madame*, you don't mind if I have another look around? What is that?"

He pointed at the piñata, which was now hanging from one of the ceiling lights with a stool underneath it looking like a hangman. Catherine pointed out the photo of Jacques she had sellotaped to the papier maché head and the darts sticking out of it, clearly showing that she had no intention of killing herself and explaining that darts was a national sport.

But everything was a potential weapon for the gendarmes and she proceeded to explain every knife that dared to be lurking in the kitchen drawer, the vitamins that looked positively lethal in their redness and even her son's discarded nerf guns.

Her exasperation soon got the better of her.

"Look I have two children and no intention of harming myself."

Unfortunately for her, the power of her statement was undermined as just then their tour of the house had brought them face to face with the Nutella sandwiches she had made out of Jacques' much-loved record collection, the amateurish red-pen photoshopping she had carried out on every photo of him, and the serial killer-like lipsticked messages of hate on the bathroom mirrors.

Her "I don't suppose you're going to pay for the window are you?" sounded pretty lame as she avoided their pitying looks and saw them to the door.

"I would not push my luck *madame*, or is that your British humour. Ha ha. We would like you to come into the gendarmerie tomorrow to write a report. Is eleven alright for you?"

Catherine sighed and agreed to it but was seething at Jacques for blowing this up out of all proportion. He really was making a Mont Blanc out of a Blancmange. She slammed the door after them and leant back against it and slid to the floor. He hadn't just ruined their marriage, he had now even managed to spoil her evening, dashed that first hint of hope she had glimpsed since all of this destruction had begun.

The question was whether he was doing it because he really was worried about her or was he just out for revenge. He had certainly got the boy scouts on his side to go by the reaction from the gendarmes. She'd never been Girl Guide material but she doubted whether a Divorcing badge was up for grabs anyway. She'd just have to find her own way out of the wilderness.

CHAPTER 15

Catherine had never been summoned to a police station before. There had been that jokey moment in her youth on a dull night out back home when two policemen had picked up a friend and her in their police car and given them a tour of the station in between receiving complaints about seagulls breaching the peace and giving warnings to young farmers for taking sheep into town in their car boots and releasing them into the pub on a Saturday night. But being on the wrong side of the law, although in a clear case of miscarriage of justice, was a new one for her. Hey that was another perversion Jacques was guilty of.

From the outside she looked like the middle-class, respectable pillar of society she was. On the inside she felt like Jessica Rabbit getting ready to come face to face with Judge Doom.

Something was causing hilarity inside the station. A group of three gendarmes were standing there and she distinctly heard the word Nutella. She didn't think they were talking about what they'd had for breakfast.

"I'm glad someone finds my situation funny," she managed to say in French before presenting herself at the desk.

Three of the men made a sheepish exit. The desk officer sobered up enough to acknowledge her presence.

"Ah Madame Dupont. Thank you for coming. Our chief would like to speak to you. Follow me."

The Chef de Gendarmerie was a slight man in his late fifties. He didn't get up from his desk when Catherine walked in but sat there on his Republican throne under the watchful eye of an official photo of the French President trying to embody the values of the State, his jacket buttons clearly straining under the effort.

"So you are the woman who has been causing us so many problems, costing us too much money in our search for you."

Catherine was amazed, not least at his English, and decided to charm him a bit, going into gushing mode.

"Oh thank God you speak English, and very good English if I may say so."

But then what he had said actually hit her... "What there was actually a search warrant out for me? A bit exaggerated don't you think?"

"Madame, your husband was very worried. He calls me here in a panic, says you are separated, that you are alone in the house, doing the *femme hysterique* and threatening to kill yourself. He was at the other side of the country and so he called us. You were not answering, you were not home, we checked, there was no car and so, *oui*, we sounded the alert. He gave us a description, he said that you were very *belle*, *madame*, you should have heard him. He was crying as he described how beautiful you were. He was so scared to lose you. Ah! You all make us suffer ...."

With that he gazed with a certain spasm of pain crossing his face at the photo on his desk of a rather ugly, fat woman who was probably very apt at commandeering Commandant Varenne as soon as he stopped over the threshold.

The thought of his wife clearly did nothing to help her case and as soon as he snapped out of his domestic musings he launched into a tirade against Catherine for wasting police time.

"*Madame*, you forced us to disturb the *préfét* during his *aperitif dinatoire*" to ask for authorisation to deploy all our resources. Just imagine. One minute you are peacefully popping the olives into the mouth, savouring your *saucisson* and the next you have to deal with *une Anglaise* who has the problem with ze French men. Who threatens to kill herself and then goes to the cinema! We all know that you love our French films *madame*, but that is no reason to star in your very own film noir!"

The mood in the room darkened as Catherine told *Monsieur le Gendarme* in no mean terms that he should be saying all this to her ex-husband. After all, he was the one who had phoned them and wasted their time. He was the one behind all of this but somehow she was getting all of the blame and ending up with a bill for a broken window to boot.

He was not to be swayed, clearly being also partial to the "fraternity" aspect of the French state's motto.

"*Madame*, I do not know what relations are between you and your husband but he was obviously very worried about you and it is not up to us to handle, how you say, your private bits. They should remain behind closed doors. They are your *jardin secret*. It is a serious matter. Death is not to be taken lightly."

Catherine decided to give "*liberté d'expression*" a run for its money seeing as gender equality was clearly not going to cut it with this dinosaur.

"Well, all of your gendarmes obviously thought that my marriage was to be taken lightly, and my divorce, the way they were laughing about it."

"Men will be men *madame*."

This stoked her fire even further, she was starting to enjoy this tussle with the French authorities.

"Yes you've said it. Men will be men. But it takes a real man to stand up for a woman against a man."

The *Anglaise* was now really starting to get on the Commandant's nerves and while showing off the English he had picked up during his exchange with his counterparts in Birmingham as part of a European cooperation programme had been fun to start with, it was getting a bit tiring, she didn't even have the same accent. His rumbling stomach was also preventing him from searching for the right words.

"Madame, please go and see one of my gendarmes who will write out the report. I hope that in future I will not need to use so much, how do you say, manpower, to localise you."

Catherine got up and looked down at him, still seated in his self-satisfied manner behind his desk.

"Oh don't worry. In future, it's all going to be about womanpower."

And without so much as an *au revoir*, hoping that she would never have the displeasure of his company ever again, she turned on her heels and was frogmarched away by the gendarme posted at the door to block any escape attempt to become a character in the annals of French police history.

CHAPTER 16

After an afternoon of phoning emergency window replacement services and perfecting the wording of her insurance claim, not having found a tick box for "Forced police entry due to dumped French husband", and an evening of picking up the pieces of her shattered life picture, one that was becoming one-flash short of a mugshot, the following day saw Catherine relishing her freedom in the great outdoors.

And great it was. Florence, her friend and neighbour, had called an emergency meeting as soon as she had spotted Catherine striding back from the gendarmerie. She had seen the officers leaving the house the previous night with their lights flashing and pounced on an opportunity for fresh gossip to give her some relief from the torpid boredom of her day.

Catherine had taken them through every detail of the previous few days, every detail except for Romain. He had taken a bit of a back seat after the gendarme episode and she didn't quite know what to make of him or his proposal. He had seemed like a nice guy but she was scared that her friends, lovely as they were, would quickly turn him into a potential suitor and having a gaggle of grown women giggling as she talked to him in the school car park was not something she could envisage as of yet.

Florence had laid on every cure for the post-traumatic stress she imagined her neighbour had endured at the hands of her fellow countrymen and was treating Catherine and their American friend

Anne to medicinal mojitos and therapeutic women's magazines by the landscaped pool.

Leafing through the pages upon pages of photos of French and international starlets dangling off yachts and comparing the abs and the abs-nots, Catherine had a revelation.

"Now I know why French women are thin," she declared.

Having clearly come to the same conclusion, Anne was quick on the draw despite her Texan drawl.

"Because they're scared their husbands are going to cheat on them."

Florence was having none of it.

"Nonsense, it's the French diet darling … and we smoke."

Catherine continued to get things off her bikini-clad chest.

"And I know why they're all on anti-depressants."

The double act with Anne continued.

"Because they KNOW their husbands are cheating on them."

"*N'importe quoi*. It's existential *angst*. You philistines have no idea how difficult it is just to be."

Catherine had no truck with Florence's vestiges of sixth form philosophy lessons. "Well you obviously have a good idea of how difficult it is just to have!"

"How capitalist! You and your obsession with possession. We're socialists darling," she paused to take a sip of her champagne-laced cocktail, "we share our riches."

"But that's the thing. I don't want to say that I HAVE a husband. I just want to say WE ARE a couple. That's the difference. I can't believe Jacques turned out to be just like all the others."

They spent the next few minutes in contemplative silence, the only sound, except for the sucking and slurping of the swimming pool filter, being the flitting of pages exposing the mistresses and misdemeanours of French politicians and international actors. Had Jane Austen been French, she wouldn't have had to look far for a title.

With rising frustration as she looked at these people who had more than most people could possibly dream of, healthy children, a roof over their head, jobs, friends, not to mention money and the trappings of power, her tutting gave way to a rant.

"I just thought I had it all. That it was all under control. Not perfect. But contained. Equal. Balanced. Same wavelength. Going in the same direction. All that shit. That I had it covered. That he respected my life and needs and I respected his. The perfect feminist vision."

Florence looked at her with something verging on pity.

"Darling, a feminist is someone who wears the pants in her own home. What men want is the post-feminist vision."

Anne's curiosity was piqued.

"Why, what does a post-feminist do?"

"The post-feminist wears the hot pants in her own home."

"I thought we were beyond that." said Catherine.

Florence looked at her over her Dior sunglasses.

"Men are never beyond hot pants. Remember that next time."

With those words of wisdom, the three friends turned over to brown their backs and lull over the conversation.

Catherine tried to imagine in what circumstances wearing hot pants on her two-child hips would have prevented her husband from straying. Anne was discretely googling to see where she could find some and how quickly they could be delivered and Florence was wiping away a tear at the thought of the pair she had recently found under the bed at the pied-à-terre she and her husband owned in Paris.

The wind started to pick up and wake them from their daydreams. Catherine was pulling her beach dress over her head when Anne put her on the spot.

"So you're certain then?"

Something about her question irritated Catherine.

"Yes, I've seen a lawyer haven't I? I've thrown him out. I'm telling everybody. But …"

"But what?"

"No, nothing …"

If she got anything more off her chest she'd have to have implants.

"I just don't get the reaction I'm getting. Like you just now, asking whether I was sure. To me it's so obvious that the trust is gone, the love is gone, the 'us' is gone. And then you get these people who look at me strangely, become uncomfortable when I say that I'm divorcing him, as if I'm the baddie in it all. I know that I'm right, after all, who on earth could stay? Why would anyone want to stay with a creepy, cheating, Machiavellian, short-arsed idiot? Except for various French actresses of course. You know, the only "oh" I ever got from him was "*eau*" de Chlamydia."

Anne and Florence looked at each other with raised eyebrows.

"Way too much information dear."

But Catherine was off again.

"But I won't live life on salad and sedatives. I want a life, not a lifestyle."

Florence was on her feet now, looking down at Catherine, disdain now dishevelling her expensively palpated and rolled face.

"Why? What makes you so special? Why shouldn't you stay for the children, for appearances, for the facility, for society, for the bloody money? Why aren't you afraid of what happens next? Of being alone? Of being shunned? Of the divorce battle?"

Anne chipped in.

"You made your bed and all that, as my mother would say …".

Catherine reacted with horror.

"Even if he unmade the bed and dirtied the sheets with another woman?!"

"Well yes," said Florence, still challenging her with one perfectly plucked eyebrow poised to unleash her truth.

"If you want to be happy, just keep your head down."

"If I keep my head down he's the only one who's going to be kept happy and I don't think he deserves it."

Catherine looked up at her two friends with new eyes, confused at the turn this time-out was taking. She got up, shoved her towel into her beach bag and turned on them, the hurt making her sound like a scratched Aretha Franklin vinyl.

"And you know why I won't put up with it? Because of another of your "made in France" products, second only to adultery in terms of net exports. Because I'm bloody well worth it."

With that she turned around and marched down the gravelled driveway back to her house. Not being a model in a cosmetic advert, her hair wasn't swinging seductively but hanging damply and limply down her face and the uniform tan of the glossies was replaced by the patchy redness of her sunburn and pin-stripes of the recliner but, hey, she hoped the drama was still there.

She sighed. Another day. Another exit.

CHAPTER 17

September usually meant a return to routine, back to basics. Not so much a new start as a resumption of repetition. This year, the record had been changed. She felt different, Catherine mused as she drove through town to fetch the children on their first day back.

That morning she'd had the impression of photobombing the picture of family life of the school run. There was no kissing dad goodbye before rushing to the car, late as ever, to make it to school by the bell. There was no skipping happily between two strong parental hands towards the new classroom. There wasn't even a half-hearted promise that papa would be picking them up that evening.

She had even avoided the groups of mummies standing around their prestige cars like white-stiletto-clad girls dancing around their handbags at an eighties disco. But even without looking she could feel the bullets of gossip randomly being shot by the snide snipers whizzing past her ears. One of them had her name on it.

She was going to have to face them again at pick up and so was in no rush now as she navigated the city streets. Her writing had been her hideout as the summer had drawn to an end, each individual letter a grain in the sand into which she had happily pushed her head. Now out in the streets, real life was forcing her to open her eyes to things she had never noticed before. It was as if she had woken up in another dimension.

In this world, hotel doorways became peopled by daytime adulterers looking over their shoulders as if under watch. Billboards were full of impossibly beautiful people marketing matches made in microcomputers. Café terraces were segregated into couples right out of a Doisneau photograph, the single Romantics who still believed in chance encounters over chequered cloths and the voyeurs for whom life was one long spectator sport but who seldom clinched a match. It was a world painted by the piercing pink of the sex shops that faded into the powder pink of the baby stores in a chronological colour chart.

As she stopped at the lights, she looked at a sweet elderly couple walking hand in hand across the zebra crossing. She shut her eyes to repel the twinge of nostalgia for a future already lost.

Opening them again she didn't know whether to laugh or cry at the sight of another old biddy pulling the randy old rascal away and holding the other woman's purple rinse wig in her hand.

"God I think they actually enjoy it," She concluded.

She drove into the school car park in a bit of a panic after her anthropological adventures. The time had come to cross it with her head held high despite her summer of humiliation. She was so wrapped up in this thought that she didn't see someone come up behind her as she grabbed her handbag from the passenger seat and again failed the cool test when she turned around.

"*Ah bonjour! C'est vous!*"

"*Bonjour!* It is the, how do you say it, the damsel in distress? But who does not look so distressed any more. She is turning into Cinderella."

Catherine giggled in embarrassment at Romain's enthusiastic greeting.

"And like Cinderella you slipped out of the cinema at midnight, not even leaving me with a glass slipper, not even a pair of Manolos or Loboutins. And you did not even call your knight in shining armour. Ah you modern women. Are we not charming enough for you? Or are you back with your evil prince?"

He added just the right amount of campness to get away with his rather forward second encounter. She laughed.

"No, I'm not back with my evil prince. No happy ending for me..."

"What do you mean ending? This is only the beginning. You are young, beautiful but you will not be like Sleeping Beauty hidden for a hundred years behind the impenetrable thorns of the dark forest of your tragic destiny."

Catherine could feel the gossipmongers going into overdrive.

"Stop. Stop. I'm not falling for that Gallic charm again."

"Gallic? Hey that was pure Disney."

Catherine managed to pour cold water on his flames though, once again showing that she still wasn't ripe for the rebound.

"It's still in the realm of make-believe though and I've just had quite a reality check."

Romain took her hand and Catherine was sure she heard a collective gasp from the far end of the car park.

"Don't give up on love and romance, *madame*, it would be such a waste."

With that he was gone and Catherine was left to collect herself. But just as she was about to resume her walk of shame, she heard him shout after her.

"Do you still have my number?"

When she nodded he shouted back.

"You see ... not even superman gives out his mobile number. You have to find him in a telephone booth."

It was a good thing that she didn't try to phone him there and then, all lines within a hundred metre radius being jammed by the rumours and gossip that were already making the rounds, giving the professional mums extra homework on their first day back.

***

Half an hour later though, still sitting in the driver's seat as the children jumped out of the car to see what was to be had for their favourite meal of the day, the sacred '*goûter*', her excitement got the better of her. She punched in his number and almost before he could answer gushed her gratitude.

"I can't thank you enough. You've made me laugh twice in a month. It's quite an achievement."

His answer was warm as ever.

"The pleasure is all mine. I just want to prove to you that some frogs can be princes."

Catherine scrunched up her eyes in embarrassment at what was already coming out of her mouth.

"To find that out I would have to kiss you and I think that's a bit premature."

"And you could end up with a queen rather than a prince," he quizzically answered. "Anyway I was suggesting nothing of the kind. I am even sure that there is some law against flirting between parents at the same school. But enough messing around, I was going to call you. Let me take you to dinner tomorrow in a heavenly place. You can get to know me better. Much better."

Catherine's answer was surprisingly curt.

"Let me call you back."

Romain was left looking in puzzlement at his phone.

Catherine's head was half way inside her handbag. She emerged with a black address book, a remnant of the P&P age, as she referred to it, when Pen and Paper meant that scribbled names and numbers had to survive the challenges of ripping, scrunching, fading and binning. She flicked through it desperately and stopped at a page, blew off the dust and texted feverishly. She then sat there tapping her fingers nervously on the steering wheel until interrupted by the noise of an incoming message like the sound of a letter landing on a mat.

She punched the air in victory, forgetting that she was in the car and ending up leaving her knuckle print in the SUV's ceiling, shook her hand to wave away the pain and phoned Romain.

"I've found a babysitter. Where is this heaven on earth?"

"I'll pick you up in my chariot at eight. Text me your address."

And with that she had a date.

Catherine still couldn't move, and not even the thought of the children wiping chocolate-pasted hands over linen sofa covers could make her budge. Right, she thought to herself, I'm going out for dinner with a man who isn't my husband, isn't my brother, isn't my cousin, isn't a colleague or my boss. How the hell do I act, what do I say, how do I eat, sit, laugh, breathe? What the hell am I doing? And more to the point. What the hell do I wear?

CHAPTER 18

Manon and Arthur were watching the screen of the security camera with the same wide-mouthed awe as they did the big screen in the multiplex cinema down the road. Nothing that the baby sitter could suggest could entice them away from it. *Maman* had spent the early evening in her en-suite bathroom as they made up dirty words with their alphabet spaghetti.

When she came out she looked pretty. No, she was always pretty. She looked really, really pretty. The jeans had been traded in for a passe-partout little black dress, the cavernous handbag for a sparkly clutch and the cowboy boots for confidence-boosting stilettoes.

With a bright red lipstick mark on their cheeks, the two were now watching this Party Barbie mummy, as Manon thought of her, close the gate and turn towards the waiting car. Their friend's father was coming out of it and towards their mother. With baited breath they monitored every move as he chastely put a peck on her cheek and guided her towards the passenger door.

Then they were gone and all they could see out on the street through the security camera was the neighbour's cat scampering past on the other side of the road.

* * *

The car purred away, down through the golden hills necklacing the city, into the cobbled streets of the old town and then up through the narrow roads clinging onto the hillside to a plateau with spectacular views over the urban lights below. The restaurant's dark side was buried in the rock just below the summit while its glazed façade seemed to hover precariously over the void. A leap of faith. Good choice, thought Catherine.

Ever the gentleman, Romain rounded the car to take her arm after handing the keys to the *voiturier* and led his princess into this contemporary turret. In his close-fitting suit and shiny black shoes he looked every inch the modern knight.

Catherine felt comfortable with him and walked into the restaurant by his side with a smile on her face. It was a while since she had been given the red carpet treatment. These days she seemed to spend more time hoovering them or just being treated like a doormat, so she was out to have a good time, whatever.

The 'whatever' moment came sooner than she had expected. She only just had time to catch a glimpse of the minimalist décor and the noise of the clinking glasses in the hushed surroundings when she found herself enveloped in the sweet embrace of the head chef, who greeted her like an old friend, "Catherine, I have heard so much about you. I'm Max. Welcome to my *chez moi*."

Her mood soured slightly when he unclasped her and gave Romain a full-blown kiss on the lips. Her escort didn't recoil in the slightest but looked over at her around the chef's hat with those eyes still twinkling and his half-ensconced mouth still smiling.

Why of course, the signs had all been there, the references to fairy god mothers, to queens, even the stereotypical sartorial savvy. And she had felt so comfortable with him, never fantasised about him, simply enjoyed his company and his unthreatening charm.

"Have to pop back to the kitchen. There's no Michelin without me. Take a seat and I'll send over the champagne," said Max blowing them both kisses.

She admitted defeat graciously and took Romain's hand, shaking her head with a smile.

"Why didn't you tell me? It looks as if you've gone through even more soul-searching than I have."

"I just wanted to get to know you better before I told you that I'd left my wife for a man. I didn't think you were ready for it. But the other day at school you just looked different to all those packs of hyenas sniffing the air for blood in the car park and I thought it was about time I told you. I hope this softens the blow," he said sweeping the room and view with his hand.

"Don't you start being arrogant as well," she gently teased him. "One lost, ten found as you say in France."

He raised the glass of champagne that had discretely arrived at their table, "And I drink to the tens of lucky men who will be queuing up to get to know you better," he said with a wink.

The rest of the evening was spent telling their respective stories. Catherine heard how Romain had struggled for years to come out, afraid of the effect on his two children, gutted at the thought of hurting his wife. When he discovered that she was having an affair earlier that year he had decided that the time was ripe and that he could minimise the devastation for all concerned.

He then listened as Catherine told him about her shattered dreams, how she had probably married the wrong man, for the wrong reasons but had counted her blessings nevertheless and tried to live according to her values regardless until the discovery of his infidelity. After all she had two beautiful, healthy children, a roof over her head and she was an owner, among the high-street staples, of a D&G dress bought for a 70% discount in the sales. She couldn't complain.

But she had been playing a role for years, finding her reality only in the fiction of her writing. After six months she had known that her husband was not to be depended on as he flitted from one job to another and, after the birth of their two children, she had the feeling of having three for the price of two. And it wasn't a bargain offer. With each passing year she had waited for him to age like a fine wine but, with growing despair, had come to the realisation that you couldn't make Pommard with plonk.

She told him why she couldn't take on the role of Mother Courage and just shut up and stay for the sake of the children or for appearances, having used up all her sacrifice cards before the discovery in her efforts to make her marriage work, to make the best of a bad decision. After all, happiness was relative, wasn't it? She had nothing more to give. He had taken it all.

Then the truth, the whole truth, and nothing but the truth came out. It had been a relief. Yes, a relief to have an excuse to leave him. Finding out about the other woman had been a godsend. She was free. The only problem was that freedom was incredibly scary. She had become so used to her shackles that she no longer knew what she could expect beyond the open door.

Romain took her hand protectively as she described the feeling of being released back into the wild like a zoo-bred animal who no longer knew how to cope with the jungle she had discovered. She felt the weight fall off her shoulders. After being hounded by those pent-up feelings of guilt, chased by the images projected by her over-fertile imagination and trapped in the dense undergrowth of social conventions, she finally felt that Romain offered her a creeper to cling to and rise above the forest of camouflaged foes to the safety of her own truth.

A few bottles of the sommelier's best vintages later, having been regaled by Max's stories, reassured by the happy outcome both men seemed to be experiencing and released from the pressure to date again, the mere thought of which sent shivers down her spine, Catherine had been dropped back home and was contentedly walking down her garden path.

However, the night was not to finish on new beginnings but on old scores. Just as she was about to close the door she felt a hand hold it open. Jacques had obviously been waiting for her return outside the house. Before she had time to react, he blocked it with his foot and spat out his envy.

"So who did you spend the evening with?"

She owed him no explanation but the words were out before she could stop them.

"No one, just a friend."

"Which friend? I know all your friends."

"I thought I knew all yours as well, but obviously not your special friends."

"You can't do this to me, you're still my wife. I want to come back. You are the most beautiful woman in the world, the most intelligent, the wittiest, the most wonderful of cooks, the best lover..."

Unfortunately for Jacques, the babysitter chose that point to emerge from the TV room, looking rather embarrassed. Unfortunately for Catherine, the babysitter happened to be called Tom.

"That's new, not just going out during the week but leaving my children with male babysitters!"

Catherine ignored Tom's presence, who hovered there, not really wanting to go without his pay but wishing he was anywhere except in the middle of this domestic.

"Well on your 'business' trips you were obviously having a good time, so now it's my turn. I'm not waiting any more. I've waited at home for you like an obedient dog for too long. I'm starting to live again. They say you only live once. But hey this pussy has nine lives."

Not having downed copious amounts of Burgundy, Jacques' brain was sharper.

"Do you mean what I think you mean?"

But Catherine was too busy taking the cat out of the bag to care.

"You tell me! You're the cat lover! What I mean, Jacques, is that you made a dog's dinner of our marriage. I'm jumping ship but I'm hoping to land on my feet like …." Her increasingly cloudy brain wasn't helping her oratory skills … "like bloody catwoman."

She then collapsed in giggles at the look on Jacques' face and at the sight of the babysitter with his eyes closed, his hand half-hiding his face as if playing hide-a-seek with a toddler, pretending he wasn't there.

"Miaow," said Jacques and left, slamming the door behind him.

Sobering up slightly and realising that Tom was still there, she pulled a few notes from her handbag, more than enough to cover her embarrassment, and pushed them into his hand while opening the door.

He thanked her and suggested, with a wink, that she might want, or need, to pop in for a coffee in the morning.

***

Catherine had hoped to see Romain on the school run the next day but it must have been the mother's turn, as he was nowhere to be seen. However, a few hostile vibes could definitely be felt as she passed one group of impeccably blow dried and designer clad mums.

Eager to make up for the rather unfortunate end to the evening she decided to send him a Skype message as soon as she got home.

Catherine: I just wanted to thank you for last night. I had a beautiful evening.

Romain: And you were beautiful company. We'll have to go back there for dinner again. Max will be more than happy to see you.

Catherine: He's a great chef. And you make a great couple.

Romain: Like you, I spent a long time living a lie. But *chérie*, we have a second chance. The other life was just a dress rehearsal. The show must go on … and this is your time to shine. If I could come out of the shadows onto the stage, then so can you.

Catherine: Thank you Romain. You're a brick.

Romain: A brick? Is that an insult or flattery? My English isn't that good!

Catherine: Put it this way, you're helping my reconstruction. See you soon.

Romain: Whenever you want *ma grande*. Just consider me as the architect of your new life.

She was about to get down to work when she heard another message arrive.

Jacques: So who are you Skyping?

Oh God, Jacques again. But his comment made her look back over her shoulder and out of the window as if he was still lurking there.

Catherine: How do you know I'm skyping?

Jacques: *Putain*, don't you know anything? You have to put it on invisible if you don't want me to know you're online.

Catherine: You could have told me before. I could have checked up on which contacts you were importing into our life. She probably uses the connected icon like a prostitute uses a red light in her window in Amsterdam to say she's available.

She immediately switched her status to invisible and shut the shutters and curtains, just in case.

CHAPTER 19

The separation had entered its ninth week. The high drama seemed to be over. She was taking her distance from her destructive relationship with her best friend the toilet bowl as the adjectives gut-wrenching, sickening and stomach-churning gradually faded from her vocabulary. Not that they had been replaced by any mellower life soundtrack. It was just a void most of the time, a going-through-the-motions existence as she waited to be in a position to take any adult decisions. Unfortunately, never had she felt less like a grown-up.

A second youth was probably not the best way of describing her new-found life motto but with Romain's help she continued to catch glimpses of the promise that life seemed so intent on tucking away in a never-ending game of happiness hide and seek.

With Max tied up at the restaurant most nights, Romain seemed only too happy to be her new platonic paramour and he wined and dined her as she fed him with her tales of her old life as a struggling writer, both filling the gaps in the other's timetables as they waited for the end of the shift, Max's shift in the kitchen, and her shift as a married woman.

She didn't know what she would have done without him, she thought as she went through the house to go and get ready for her weekly jog with her friends. Changing into her shorts and top, she caught sight of her body in the dressing room mirror. She wasn't quite as scrawny as she'd been a few weeks ago, she thought, studying her figure. Her appetite had certainly come back the previous night as she'd worked her way rapturously through the autumn tasting menu, the earthy ceps with melting *foie gras*, the subtle hazelnut and ricotta filled ravioli, the flamboyant blood-orange hues of the pan-roasted duck and *écrasé* of squash. Now she just needed to tone up in readiness for the boxing match that lay ahead with her new sparring partner.

Carefully locking the door behind her, she jogged gently down the hill to the lake where Anne and Flo were waiting for her. Her poolside outburst a few weeks ago had been laid to rest. Her nerves had been riding high, her friends could understand that, and if there was one thing that was beyond comparison, it was relationships. You could compare suntans, waist size, nails, homes, cars and holidays but there was no benchmark when it came to marital states. Without a lie test, in particular a lying-to-yourself test, and camera, infra-red to pick up the sweat marks, who knew what went on behind domestic doors.

"So how's the infidel these days?" Anne got to the point. "Seen him?"

"He's been behaving a bit weirdly. As if he's seen the light. Found religion. He's just nice all the time, and that is just not him, I mean, he's French."

"Thanks a lot *chérie*!" said Florence, looking impeccable as usual in her pink designer running gear

"You know what I mean, you don't really go in for all that "have a nice day" fake smile stuff. You just shrug, poof and grunt and say that at least you're not being a hypocrite...

Anne couldn't help herself.

"They do wham, bang, thank you ma'am quite well though...."

Catherine glared at her.

"Thanks for the reminder. And he's just being kind all the time, turning up to take my car for a service, popping up unexpectedly to take the children out, that kind of thing ... oh hold on", she interrupted her rant as her phone told her a text message had arrived, checking just in case it was the school or urgently work-related.

"Oh speak of the *diable*. It's him. Oh my God…"

Catherine read out the message.

"I have proof that you are cheating on me. What kind of woman are you? You are the mother of my children, you should be the Madonna, mother of Jesus, not Madonna who goes out with Latin American dancers called Jésus. How was the Michelin starred restaurant with tall, dark and handsome last night?"

"How the hell did he know about that?" she feverishly texted him back. The answer was immediate.

"Oh *merde*," she said as she showed the screen to her fellow runners.

"Maybe you shouldn't have entered the address into the sat nav ma chérie."

"It's like being in some kind of creepy stalker film," said Anne aghast.

"Looks more to me like he's two steps ahead of you all the time," pointed out Florence.

"You're right," said Catherine, "and for a guy with such short legs…."

So much for being nice. He had just been checking up on her. How dare he turn the tables on her like that! He was the lying, cheating bastard and now he was trying to make out that she was the femme fatale. Catherine turned her head to hide the tears that were pooling in her eyes from her friends. She felt watched, used, spied upon. She'd been had, was gradually being turned into the bad guy in some kind of sick thriller.

"See that duck," she said, pointing out over the water. "That's me since the divorce, head in the water and arse in the air, fishing for answers, not knowing what's going on around me."

"And you've been well and truly ducked dear," Anne patted her back with a hint of a told-you-so in her smile.

Catherine broke into a sprint, just wanting to run away from it all. A few hundred metres later she was panting on the picturesque little pontoon when the other two caught up with her.

Florence put her arm around her.

"Calm down *ma poule*. I have an idea. We have to ... how do you say ... win him at his own match ..."

The other two women looked at her uncomprehendingly before the penny finally dropped.

"You mean beat him at his own game!"

"Yes, that's it. If he has that much time to waste, then let's start really wasting his time."

The three huddled together on the jetty, indifferent to the autumnal damp of the wood beneath them and listened to Flo's master plan. By the time they'd fine-tuned the details their sweat had grown cold and the chill was seeping into their skin. They stood up shivering to run back to their respective homes. With a last defiant look back at that duck mooning at her in mockery, Catherine picked up a stone and threw it in its direction. It missed its mark but the ripples she had set off disrupted his hunt and, disgruntled, he toppled backwards onto the surface of the water and slunk away in a huff.

CHAPTER 20

Game on. Jacques was so intent on playing his own little games with his estranged wife that he had no idea that he'd turned into a pawn in hers. Not at first at least.

A few days after taking the car for the alleged MOT, Jacques was back at the marital home. He was already getting tired of staying in his friend's pool house. The pool wasn't even heated and the arrival of autumn had put pay to any hopes he'd had of lounging out his wife's hysterics in style. A pool house without a useable pool was basically a granny flat, not quite as appealing.

This time he'd told Catherine that he needed the SUV's boot to go and stock up with a few bachelor necessities in Ikea, hoping that the pathos of his situation would buy him the sympathy vote. She'd simply thrown the keys at him and slammed the door in his face. But it didn't matter, he had no intention of spending the day putting together jigsaw furniture. He had laid out other plans.

As soon as he could park the car out of sight of the house he turned on the sat nav and started analysing all the addresses entered since he'd last driven it. He'd caught her out last time! What was his world coming to? Her going to flashy restaurants with other men while his dinner choices were usually a can of tuna or McDonald's!

Let's see where she'd been this time. He saw an address that he didn't recognise, took a photo of the screen with his smartphone for future evidence, switched on the engine and followed the directions.

After half an hour or so he found himself in a part of the city he didn't often go to. It was the other side of the station in a neighbourhood far removed from the bourgeois surroundings of his leafy suburbs. He parked right in front of the street number Catherine had entered into the sat nav.

It was a nondescript building with blacked out windows and a small sign above the door with the words "*La vie en rose*" like the Piaf song. He was disappointed, it was probably just where she went for one of her Zumba classes. Or a dance studio for Manon. Seeing as he was there and parked he decided to go in and check though … just in case the teacher was a waxed off, sexed up Brazilian who was giving her private tuition after hours.

He rang the discrete doorbell. It unlocked with a click and he pushed it open. It was dark inside; classes couldn't have started yet but there seemed to be a bar down at the bottom of a long corridor with a line-up of doors on each side. He'd been expecting another kind of barre. What the hell was she doing coming to a place like this?

Nervously, he started walking down the shadowy corridor, gradually hearing doors open and shut behind him. By the time he'd reached the counter and saw the black studded cap of the man standing behind it, it was too late. When the barman turned around to take down the bottle of Southern Comfort from the shelf behind him, displaying his cut-out trousers, he knew that this wasn't the kind to place to come and dance cheek to cheek, at least not the cheeks he was used to.

Turning to make his escape before anyone could ask him what his tipple was, he came face to face with four or five muscle-rippling types with handlebar moustaches who were eyeing him up like a Harley in a motorbike store. He took a step back but was caged in by the bar. By now the sweat was escaping from his body like water through a colander. He hoped that he was sending out the right vibes. Or did the smell of fear turn them on?

He squirmed as one of the burly bikers took a new-leather sounding step towards him, a hungry smile on his face, and started touching the expensive material of his Boss suit. He definitely wasn't in charge of things now, and he started to have images of himself strapped to the walls of one of the rooms behind the doors, ending his life as a sex slave to one of these gentlemen.

When Mr Touchy Feely said "so are we going to toss for him?" he decided he wasn't going to be a biker babe for anyone and dived under the legs of the guy in front of him and made a mad dash for the door. He thanked God when he found it was open and, without a backward glance, he was out of it and back in the blinding light of the street. He jumped into the SUV, bolted it and drove off in a riotous shrieking of tyres.

***

Back in "*La vie en rose*", the barman had just got off the phone, confirming that the job was done, and was already serving his regulars a round of *kir royal* on the house. "Flo says thanks," he said as he went back to dusting his framed photo of Mylène Farmer.

***

After that episode, Jacques was determined to keep an even closer eye on his wife. By now he'd come to suspect her to be strange and not just estranged. Had she been living a double life as well?

The scepticism was only too visible in her eyes when he asked to borrow the car again to go to the dump with his empty Ikea cartons a few days after recovering from his close encounter of the third kind but he ignored it, too curious to see where the sat nav would take him this time.

The church hall he was guided to looked rather more wholesome than his last destination so he walked in without any real suspicion, musing to himself that it was more probable that Catherine came here for one of her charity events than to take the priest's virginity in the vestry.

There seemed to be some kind of meeting going on and before he knew it he was accosted, kindly this time, by a man of his age who steered him adroitly to the one of the spare seats set out in a circle with an understanding look on his face.

So that was it! His wife was a secret alcoholic and she was coming here for group counselling sessions! He was only half-listening to the testimonials but after looking around to see whether any of the participants could be one of her secretive dinner dates he suddenly noticed that every single one of them were men. It was only then that he realised that the words that had been bandied about for the past ten minutes or so, "abstinence" and "lack of control", "dysfunction", "relationship breakdown" and "depression" weren't being used to describe their shot-downing capacities but their sexual performances.

Looking around in a rather unfortunate panic, that very emotion the group was trying to avoid, he saw the notice posted up on the noticeboard behind the group leader "Premature Ejaculators Anonymous". With that he was up in no time and made rather a quick withdrawal himself.

"That didn't take you long," said Catherine when he handed back the keys only half an hour later. He could have been mistaken, but he was sure that the scepticism had been replaced by a concealed amusement.

After following two more leads over the next two weeks that saw him struggle for what seemed like hours from the mangle-like grips of some heavily tarnished golden oldies at a tea-dance in an old people's home and spend two hours trying to escape from the folds of a sect that believed that God would appear to them through the constant wearing of sunglasses, he came to two conclusions. Either Catherine had a very eclectic taste when it came to hobbies or he was being given the run-around.

Not wanting to answer any questions about what exactly he'd had to do to escape the sect's initiation ceremony without anyone noticing that one body, naked barring the goggles, was missing from the circle of sunbeds, he decided to drop the sat nav as an espionage device and get the dirt on his wife some other way.

CHAPTER 21

"Oh *chèrie*, Loulou and his little friends were laughing so much about it that one almost choked on his peanut. Loulou had to get right behind him and give him the Heimlich. Thank God Jacques had gone by then, imagine the Heimlich in cut-out trousers!"

Catherine could hardly speak she was laughing so hard. It got worse when Anne chipped in.

"And Father Paul said that he was so keen to get out of that church hall incognito that he grabbed a hymn book and hid his face all the way out to the car. He'd never seen such shame outside of a confession box!"

The morning coffee ritual with her two friends had never been such fun. Jacques was keeping them entertained with his weekly run of riotous revenge tactics. The divorce was turning into a scream. In the hysterical gaggle of girlfriends on a night out sense of the word.

After ordering another round of drinks from Tom, who was enjoying watching Catherine indulge in her Chantilly-topped *chocolat chaud* instead of her usual drug of double espressos, Florence suddenly turned to Catherine with a serious look on her face.

"*Bon*, so we've got him sorted. Now it is time to get you sorted."

"What do you mean? I am sorted. I've been dumping and separating for the past four months."

It suddenly felt like an intervention when Anne deftly took up Florence's line of thought.

"Yes, my darling, but if your shelf gets any emptier, you'll find yourself on it one day."

Catherine was baffled. She thought that she was doing all right. Being a survivor. She had the kids for love, the house for warmth, the novel for meaning, Romain for nights out, her friends for company.

Florence, however, wasn't having any of it.

"But your bottom drawer is empty."

"My what? Talking to you is like flicking through a home improvement catalogue, shelves, drawers…"

Florence was getting as excited as a child on a treasure hunt.

"Ah you're getting hotter darling, but I'm not talking DIY. You've probably had enough of that over the past few months. I think you need an interior designer…" That had Anne in fits of giggles.

Catherine was wary.

"Why do I have a feeling you're not talking feng shui here?"

Anne sobered up.

"She's right though. You need to think about yourself, about your own needs, about the future, about getting back into the saddle again."

Catherine was slightly taken aback at this direct attack on her celibacy. She wasn't sure what to say. After all, she had been with the same man for almost twenty years. Did they honestly think she could just take off her clothes in front of anyone except for her gynaecologist? And that was bad enough.

"Look, just stop right there. Who would want me? Two kids, lots of mileage and one extremely careless owner."

She looked up with embarrassment as Tom, once again picking his moment, came over to wipe down their table.

Anne tapped her on the hand.

"Come on, just take one look at yourself. You're a beautiful, charming, intelligent, funny woman Catherine. Men will be queuing up for you as soon as you send out the right vibes."

"I'll second that," Tom said, who then, realising that he had been an uninvited guest in their conversation, scuttled off with an awkward smile.

Florence managed to lighten the tone.

"And four months *chérie*! How do you cope? I'd be bonking baguettes by now!"

"Remind me never to eat bread at your house again Florence! I don't know. It's like going back to the first time, like treading virgin ground…"

"Oh come on", said Florence, downing her fresh espresso with one voracious gulp. "Cut out the adolescent thing, just make sure you cut down the virgin forest, get some good lingerie and we'll take care of the rest. I feel a dinner party coming on… Right, let's strike while the ironing board is hot... Girls, we are going shopping."

***

Florence seemed to know every lingerie store owner in town, from the innocent looking old biddy with a surprising back-shop collection of black leather numbers to the hip shop that made a point of employing only men as fitters.

At the first stop she insisted on Catherine having her chest measured to avoid wasting time later. When Catherine tried to insist that she could manage on her own and didn't need some stranger boob-handling her, Flo came back with an incontestable argument.

"If you can't take your kit off in a changing room then what happens when a man gets his kit out in your bedroom."

She had a point.

The rest of the morning was spent making the rounds to dress up Catherine's cast-aside and overlooked forms in a way that would make her coveted and looked over. Decidedly, Flo was France's answer to Mae West. From the frumpy to the fun to the frankly not there, by lunchtime Catherine had gone through as many bras, bustiers and basques as a Crazy Horse showgirl on a Saturday night.

Knicker-shopping in M & S had never been this much fun, she thought, as she put down her exquisitely designed paper shopping bags with their extortionately expensive contents on her bedroom floor. She took the delicate pieces out one by one, coming back to reality as she felt each object of fantasy and tried to imagine herself living up to the sex symbol persona they were provoking her to adopt.

She looked down at the slight bulge of her stomach and couldn't think why anyone would want to passionately rip any flimsy piece of fabric off her. Looking up, her gaze fell on an old photo of her and Jacques that she'd somehow forgotten to remove from the photo mosaic on her dressing table. Angry and frustrated she grabbed the sexy black basque with matching suspender belt and threw it at the photo. It hung over it, blacking out her past, suspending her future.

CHAPTER 22

Flo's dinner parties were legendary. Led-lit, palm-tree filled pots were lined up to greet the guests picking their way up the gravel driveway in red-soled stilettoes or suede loafers they preferred not to get scuffed.

Once past the front door they entered into a pleasure ride that seemed to escape their control, guided to one of the free places, swung around to get acquainted with their companions on the Roche-Bobois, caught up in the constant background chatter, tipped from their almost reclined positions into upright dining chairs before being propelled once again back into the swirl of conversation. Stepping out of the door at the end of the evening was like being spat out of a civilised Eurodisney rollercoaster, dizzy and uncoordinated.

Despite being caught up in the whirl of trays and bottles, gusts of laughter and Spotify-sent vibes, Flo was aware that one of her guests was yet to turn up. In half a mind to march down the road to fetch her, she suddenly saw the late-arrival sneak in through the open door and discretely look around for her. Intent on making her guest the centre of attention, she got up from the table, opened her arms wide in greeting and planted a dramatic kiss on both cheeks.

"Ma petite Catherine. *Enfin.* We've been waiting for you. Come in. Come in. I've saved you a place next to Marco. He'll take good care of you."

Catherine extricated her face from Flo's immaculate blow dry and looked down at the man she was going to have to sit next to for the rest of the evening.

Flo had been over at hers twice that day to check what she was wearing that night, even what lingerie was going on underneath. She'd also phoned her twice, the first time to tell her to brush up on her Italian and the second time to warn her not to look too desperate "because men hated that". Before Catherine could tell her that she wasn't in the least bit desperate and that she was the one prepping her like a virgin on her first night at the brothel, Flo had rung off to sort out some problem with the *gougères* not rising properly for the occasion or some equally dramatic culinary development.

Marco was a fifty-something who was either just back from an Indian summer in St Tropez or from a St Tropez spray salon. He smiled. There was no doubt about it. It was the salon, as he'd obviously had his teeth buffed and polished there at the same time. Any hopes she may have had of romance were culled by the thought of him sitting there in his pod with a rugbyman's toothguard full of bleaching gel in his mouth.

He got up to pull out her chair and to physically ease her down into it. His arm remained draped around the small of her back as he parked his face in front of hers, obstructing her view of any other interesting people seated around the vast dinner table. Thankfully, his slightly inebriated neighbour on the other side chose just that moment to spill some wine over his trousers, which he wiped off huffily and at length with unconcealed annoyance. She just about had time to send an SOS signal to Flo across the table by writing 'WTF?' in her soup with croutons before he dived in once again, without bothering with the preliminaries.

"So Florence tells me you are single."

"No, I just have more fun going to dinner parties without my husband."

It took some moments for the sarcasm to travel across the international dateline and for him to get it and he just sat there taken aback for an instant.

"Aha, you are joking!" Before he checked "You are joking?"

Catherine didn't dignify the question with a reply, but returned the question.

"And where is your wife?"

He winked at her as if she had just asked the million-dollar question.

"There is no *signora*. No *bambini*," at which point he actually shuddered, "I do what I like, have what I like, anytime, anywhere. I'm an interior designer. I get into women's heads and give them what they really want."

By this time his head was practically in her *decollete*, which at least meant that she could catch Florence's eye across the table. She seemed to sense that things were hotting up between them.

"A red hot chilli pepper darling?"

"Don't you have a cocktail sausage on a prick, sorry, stick, how Freudian of me."

Florence's face dropped, her matchmaking obviously not going to light any fires that night.

"Don't you want anything to dip in your hummus?" she whispered cryptically past the other guests.

But before she could answer Marco was clearly over his cleavage-gazing and back on form.

"Don't feed her too much Florence. I'm hoping to fill her up with dessert."

That was it. The slime threshold had been crossed and the thought of ploughing her way through two more rounds of sweet nothings and acid attacks with this one was just too nauseating to consider. The pocket of her smart black trousers suddenly started to vibrate.

"Oh, do excuse me, *scusi* Marco, that's my phone."

She took out her phone with apologetic gestures towards him, and answered it, making no attempt to speak in hushed tones.

"Hi Tom."

She looked over the phone at him and mouthed "It's the baby-sitter" before resuming her conversation.

"Yes. Oh dear. Vomiting? No. Is it serious? Oh, and diarrhoea? What? All over the Italian sofa? Oh well, that's kids for you. No, don't worry. I'll be back now. As fast as I can." She switched off the phone with a long sigh.

She turned to Marco in distress.

"Oh dear, I'm so sorry Marco but my daughter's been taken ill. Yes, molto vomito everywhere it seems. I just have to go and check on her, mop it up and," with a wink at him, "I may even be back for your dessert! What do you say? Hey, you can even come and visit me sometime. I may need some help covering up the stains on the sofa."

Marco looked as if he'd just emerged from the proverbial cold shower.

"I don't really do plastic covers," he answered icily and turned his sights back to getting the last of the Bordeaux out of his shiny trousers.

Funnily enough, Catherine didn't seem that disappointed.

"Oh well, that's a pity. Florence, I'm frightfully sorry but I have to dash. Hope I haven't dashed your hopes."

Florence only frowned at her, thwarted in her attempts to set up her neighbour and get a family-and-friends discount from Marco for remodelling her kitchen. Damn. He was a good designer, though she couldn't really blame Catherine. After all, men in slippery silk clothing weren't really ones to have and to hold. She'd have to go back to the drawing board.

Across the road, Catherine was already in bed. The truth was that the children were with their father. There had been no vomit, no babysitter … and no happy outcome to the evening. She was in bed at 10 o'clock on a Saturday watching Kramer v Kramer. Again.

She didn't want her husband. She didn't want Marco. She didn't even want Dustin Hoffman. No matter how good his French toast. Who did she want? Given her reactions that evening, she obviously wasn't ready to find out. She picked up the sizzling red bra and knickers she had discarded in disgust beside the bed and threw them in frustration over the TV set.

CHAPTER 23

Florence wasn't one to give up easily. With an absent husband, student children who always seemed to be doing cushy internships at PR firms in Paris or luxury hotels in Gstaad, and someone who came in to do every possible household or garden chore, it gave her a little project between manicures, lunches and her hours-long treks to get the finest antipasti from the best Italian delicatessen in the city. Catherine was sure that the delicatessen took malign pleasure in knowing that all these rich socialites had to make such a superhuman effort to come along to his grotty little neighbourhood for the pleasure of the divine produce he sourced from his faithful old friends back in the hills of Piedmonte. He could almost hear the central locking on their overpriced runabouts as they turned off the main road along the river into his immigrant-populated arrondissement. But he knew it was worth their while. They not only got kudos for their aperitif but also for the perilous journey they had to embark on to bring the hunt back home.

Florence was on the way back from the morning adventure with a boot full of *involtini*, marinated artichokes and anchovy-filled baby peppers when she had another bright idea. She was immediately on the phone to Catherine to invite her to the Franco-British family rugby picnic she was organising the next day.

"You never know darling, there may be a lovely divorced father there looking for a bit of scrum action."

The word rugby acted on the Welsh woman like the word shopping to a Kardashian and she said yes like a shot, thinking it would be a great idea for the children to be out in the fresh air and mixing with others.

They seemed to be coping with the separation with a resilience that only children tend to show. They'd found their own survival mechanisms, identifying the friends in the same situation, turning on the tears with the teachers to avoid being told off for sloppy work and drawing up two equally long lists for Father Christmas, known to divorced parents as the Christmas guilt list. But a good old "family picnic", even if her family was amputated and only limping along at the moment, would be a good chance to show that she was not a leper and if she could find a prop while she was there, then all the better.

Armed with her hamper and picnic rug, the following day Catherine joined Florence and her other expat friends at the local park. For a late October day, the weather was glorious and the sun shone through the autumn leaves, encircling the picnickers in a blaze of colour.

The children were having a great time, running about the place with mini rugby balls, making the most of the chance to throw themselves into mud, tackle and jump on other children and just be generally boisterous between mouthfuls of cucumber sandwiches and chocolate brownies.

The women seemed to be gathered in one corner, laying out the picnic as if it was a photo shoot for Nigella's latest 'sultry summer' cookbook. Catherine hid her amateurishly unravelling Caesar salad wraps behind the icebox overflowing with bottles of rosé and sparkling water, too ashamed to display them beside the other immaculately presented Delicatessen dainties and pinterest-worthy goodies.

The conversation quickly turned from gushing over quinoa verrines and kale gazpacho to school. Catherine listened patiently as one mum performed a nifty surgical incision into the conversation to bring up her son's first-in-class ranking. Another managed to deftly implant the fact that her daughter was being pushed up a year as she was so bored with the easy-peasy curriculum.

Another shared the second opinion she had just obtained from an ortho-physio-phono-psycho-sophro-logist who had confirmed what she had known all along, that her child was not slow but picking up too much information at the same time because his brain, and the rest of his hyperactive nervous system, was working too quickly and was, in fact, so ahead of himself, of everyone else, and even of his teacher, that he was off the chart, which is why he was unable to write anything down in class or repeat what had just been said.

When Catherine said "Oh, like some kind of intellectual back to the future then," the super-child's mum just looked at her scathingly and told them how her other child was switching schools because she didn't think his teacher understood him, when in fact it was a secret to no one that he'd just been "invited to leave" for bringing his Doberman puppy into school in his school bag as his personal "guard dog".

Catherine's mind started wandering and she turned her attention to the dads finishing off their rugby sevens match. Catherine had done her maths. There were no single dads. Matching the husband to the wife hadn't been difficult and there had been none left over.

One of the dads started shouting at the children to come over so that they could put together a mixed team. The older ones ran along, leaving the toddlers to make mud pies, and Catherine was thrilled to see her two run over enthusiastically. She'd done her duty as a Welsh mum.

They were missing a player to have an equal field and one of the dads shouted over at their other halves that they needed reinforcements. The other mums looked down into their rosé or pointed to their cream chinos but Catherine was up in a flash, only too glad to share the moment with the children. They cheered when they saw her dash across the field in her jeans and "Real Women Drink Beer" t-shirt and insisted she play on their team.

Catherine hadn't had such a laugh in a while. It was all rough and tumble, fortunately with more rules being broken than bones, but no one cared as they attempted scrums, belly flopped tries and high-fived with their chests as they attempted to recover the air-borne oval ball.

All the action now seemed to be on the field, a certain quiet having fallen over the WI corner beyond the coat and jumper-marked posts.

But the lineswomen were soon out in force and began disrupting the match by calling penalties and making replacements

"Charles darling, could you come and open the wine. No, now. Straight away."

"Hugo, I think the dog needs a walk. No, I can't go. I have to look after the baby. No, I don't think it can wait until after the scrum dear."

"Think of your heart Peter, you know what the doctor said about too much excitement. Come and have a nice sit down with me."

Before long most of the men had traipsed sulkily off the field, their wives having called full time on their fun and they sat there drinking their red wine as Catherine finished the game with a handful of muddy and ragged looking children.

On the way back in the car, the children nodded off and she considered the cold goodbyes she'd earned from the women and the hearty pats on the shoulder and averted eyes she'd experienced from the men. "God are they that insecure? I wasn't exactly playing rugby dressed like a Brazilian beach volley player!"

Back home, she left the children to their afternoon nap and went for a hot bath. She thought back over the afternoon as she soaped off the earth and grass marks from her elbows and arms. Apparently she'd been the most dangerous element on that field today. What were they afraid of? That she was going to take revenge on her cheating husband by luring away someone else's? And fall down to his level? Live according to his standards?

Well they were wrong. There must be plenty of young single men out there, you just had to find the right foraging grounds... a rugby ground was obviously too full of territorial tigresses. She stepped on the sports bra she'd shed on the floor as she climbed out of the bath, wincing as the clasp pierced her toe. I just hope that doesn't bring me a hundred years of man-free slumber she said as she hurled it, again in frustration, and it glided down over Jacques' proprietorial grin on the wedding photograph.

CHAPTER 24

"I'm giving you one last chance and then I'm buying ten cats and starting shopping for thermal undies at Damart," Catherine told Flo as she was kneading the bread during her weekly baking session. It was her attempt to create an Enid Blyton atmosphere for the children despite the absence of the pater familias. Unfortunately, given her frustration, the bread was getting more of a bruising and a pounding than anything else and would probably end up as flat as a KO'd boxer in a fighting ring.

Flo was over the moon. She'd been wanting to go clubbing for years but due to her husband's disinclination, her friends' preference for elegant dinners and, to put it frankly, her age, she had been forced to vent her pent-up frustration by being the relative making a laughing stock of herself at weddings. The problem was that weddings were becoming far and few between at the moment. Her generation either already so long married they could hardly remember why they had ever said yes in the first place and the next generation too attached to social media to be anyone or anything else's ball and chain.

"It's going to be fun, you'll see. We'll dance, have a few drinks and find you a toy boy. The others were too old, too married. You need something fresh, young, someone who still believes in love."

Catherine wasn't convinced. She wasn't ready to be a yummy mummy, didn't want a stepdad for the children who would be mistaken for their older brother and didn't want to pretend she knew who Calvin Harris was. But she'd made Florence promise to take her to a club where the music had words and wasn't located in some purpose-built disco on a roundabout on the way out of town, and definitely not one where French couples danced "le rock" like a 50s jive contest. Florence promised VIP treatment, champagne and dress codes and finally got Catherine to say yes.

***

Catherine couldn't believe she was actually googling "what to wear to a nightclub + France". But, surrounded by half the contents of her wardrobe that were dancing around her in some kind of revengeful reversal of fortune, she was in a panic. Flo was picking her up in a taxi in ten minutes and she had already ditched her jeans for being too grunge, her smiley T-shirt for being too techno, her miniskirt for being too pop and the rest of her wardrobe for being too easy listening.

She scrolled down through the search results but found nothing to tell her exactly how a 38-year-old of her shape and colouring should dress for a nightclub in her precise part of the world. Hearing a horn being beeped outside, she did what thousands of others were probably doing at the same time, had done before her and would surely resort to after her. She grabbed the first pair of black jeans and black top she could see, pulled on her black leather jacket and black high-heeled ankle boots and hit the town.

***

At least it had the word "Lounge" in its name, she thought to herself as she queued up along the rather pretentious red carpet to get past the bouncer, or the "physiognomist" as the French pompously insisted on calling them, at the door. Catherine was trying to prepare herself for the mortification of being turned away for being too old or for lack of street cred. The drinks she'd downed with Flo at their usual, rather more age-relevant haunts, at the city's five-star hotel bars were starting to kick in, but not enough to give Catherine that impression of a God-given right to rave or whatever she was meant to do once she was given temporary membership of this club of youth.

Of course, she wasn't really there to dance. That was Flo's plan. She was there to 'pull'. Which seemed to imply that anyone who came away with the force of her hand wouldn't be there of their own free will. Not a great start to any relationship she mused. Hey Muse, maybe they'd play that. At least she'd heard of them.

For the time being she was being pushed forward by the crowd to be subjected to the bouncer's scrutiny. He took her in with his eyes like a human airport body scanner before giving Flo the one-over. "*Allez-y Mesdames.*" God that was crushing in itself. *Mesdames*? The mark of respect that disrespectfully told them in one fell semantic swoop that they were too old for this game. For God's sake, she was more or less Kate Moss' age and if she could market "Coco Mademoiselle" then, hell, she could channel Mademoiselle as well.

***

Flo being Flo, and money being money and not in the least bit ageist, in fact, quite the opposite, they had managed to get themselves a table holding a lovely chilled bottle of champagne in its cryogenic bath that would hopefully make them feel younger with every sip.

The club was tasteful, with a boudoir vibe, if those two adjectives could ever be put together. But anyway, at least they could sit on their low poofs and watch how the others were managing to look cool before they ventured out under the spotlights.

After a few glasses, they had excitedly picked up on a song they recognised, even if it was a remix, and were displaying their eighties and nineties-honed dance moves and starting to own their piece of the dance floor.

Flo had given up pointing out potential targets to Catherine after her reaction had been only to say that beards reminded her of dead English kings and didn't she think that men who were too well groomed were bound to be a nightmare to share a bathroom with.

It was an admittedly young crowd, not quite young enough to be Catherine's children as she had announced as soon as she had handed in her coat and sussed out her fellow-clubbers, but they would admittedly have to make a bit of a quantum leap to close the age gap.

As the sparkling ambrosia seeped into all the right spots and started hitting them, none of this mattered and Flo and Catherine got down to the business of letting down their hair and trying very hard to get back their lost youth.

As she was in the middle of this worthwhile quest and showing Flo some dance moves last seen in a mid-Wales rugby club party circa 1992, one such lost youth came up behind Catherine's gradually dishevelling mane of hair and tapped her on the shoulder. She turned around defensively only to see the contemptuous cocktail of surprise and disappointment in his eyes.

"Yo cougar. Where's your leopard skin?"

Catherine turned her back on him but he came back after a quick change of tactic, probably thinking she would be easy prey for him.

"Hey, the night is young, even if you aren't. Don't you want to show me some of your tricks?"

Annoyed by his persistence Catherine snarled back at him.

"If I had any I'd make you disappear."

"Hey no need to get your claws out. I'm gone, I'm gone. *Vieille truie*. Shouldn't you be home knitting or something?"

The party was over for Catherine.

"I'm getting out of here," she shouted at Flo over the music.

Unfortunately for her, the music cut to a quiet instrumental part just, as she explained why.

"My coil is older than some of these kids."

Those around them heard her and looked over, their laughter and taunts drowned by the resumption of the anthem-like chorus. Catherine pushed her way out of the club, followed close on her heels by a defeated Flo, who at least remembered to pick up their coats. The taxi ride home was a subdued affair.

Nightclubs hadn't been a good idea, thought Flo, she's still too raw, still too thin-skinned to cope with the real world. I'd better not get her on to Tinder yet.

Catherine was still stung by the red-faced shame of being called a cougar. What was happening to her? This wasn't her. This wasn't her life. This wasn't supposed to happen. Maybe she was supposed to be home, maybe not knitting, but reading a self-improving book or watching popular cabaret programmes on the TV.

She gave Flo a short kiss on the cheek at the gate and went in without a word. There was nothing more to say. Nothing more to be done. She was too old. Out of the game. An outcast. Over the hill. That was it. It was game over.

Back in the bedroom, the basque, already recycled once in its new and unused state, this time ended up in the rubbish basket. Catherine delved into her knickers drawer and pulled out a good old plain white cotton pair that seemed more in keeping with her own worn out state. Washed out was the new black.

CHAPTER 25

Catherine was giving the French some chic for their money the next day as she shopped in the city centre. Trying to distance herself as far as possible from the cougar that had apparently stalked the dance floors the previous evening, she had put on her "grown-up clothes". A faux-Chanel jacket, smart jeans and designer sunglasses. She was just being who she was, a middle-aged, middle-class, middle-of-the-road woman indulging in a bit of comfort-shopping on her weekend without her children and without any other distraction.

She wasn't aware that she was giving out any particular vibes but, as one of her male friends put it a few days later, the bouquet of fresh divorcee meat can be picked up a mile off, or a kilometre off in this imperially-challenged country.

At first she thought that the *"Excusez-moi"* was meant for the person behind her. She carried on purposefully past the city-centre boutiques projecting their actress-named handbags on audiences who swooned only at the price tags. She even continued past the queues waiting patiently for their rationed capsules of coffee, following the orders of the suit-uniformed army of young recruits, who preached the love of the pod with the same caffeine-fuelled fervour as their Mormon counterparts tried to convert others to their god.

The second *"Excusez-moi"* drowned out her thoughts and she realised that it was meant for her. She automatically went into Girl Guide mode without giving any real attention to the person behind the voice.

"Oui, pardon, vous vouliez?"

"Ah, but you are English. Your accent is very *mignon. Ecoutez,* I'm not in the habit of doing this, but can I invite you for a coffee? This café down there makes the best espressos."

The man in front of her was in his mid-forties, well dressed in a casual, jaunty, weekend style, but without ostentation, his salt and pepper hair just the right length and thickness, his smile was shy, not smarmy and he seemed surprised himself to have had the guts to make such a proposal.

But it wasn't his day. For all intents and purposes, he could have been a torero holding up a red rag in front of her eyes. All the man-made disappointments and humiliations that had been thrown at her, all the taunts and jabs that had gored her over the past few months had her snorting and scraping the ground in anger. No one was going to take this bull by its horns.

"What is it with you all? Do I look single? Do I look available? Do I look desperate? Is there a "looking for a shag with any passer-by" sticker stuck to my forehead? This never happened to me when I was married? Do you men just walk around looking at women's wedding ring fingers? Do you think that a coffee with you is going to make me fall head over heels in love and change my existence forever? Are you going to carry me off on your trusted steed? No. I don't want a coffee with you. I just want a bit of normality and not this constant pressure to date and mate and worry about my fate."

After her tirade she marched off into a blood-stained sunset leaving the poor man lurching at his sudden-death in the afternoon experience.

He looked around, hoping that no one had seen the reaction he'd just triggered in that sweet-looking lady. She'd looked so effortlessly elegant, smart but down to earth. He couldn't help but wonder where the dragon's tongue had sprung from. Shrugging his shoulders and thinking that his beloved wife was probably telling him that it was still too early after her untimely death for him to start looking for love again, he headed off in the other direction. His stallion-studded car was parked down a side street. He got into it, missing the pleasure of sharing the thrill, and drove off with that recognisable roar, feeling even heavier at the thought that the poor woman had clearly a lot of steam of her own to vent.

The "poor woman" was soon back home thinking about the poor sod she'd turned into the scapegoat for all his fellow men today. Knowing her luck, he was probably the love of her life and she'd just sent him off with his tail between his legs.

The truth was that she was scared. Just very, very scared.

CHAPTER 26

The late autumn mists were draped like a white fox stole around the hills of the Beaujolais. Stripped bare of their flaming leaves that had alerted the vintners to harvest season, the empty vines now simply studded the hills like the forehead of an overenthusiastic piercer.

Jacques' modern company car ripped its way through this grey and white landscape, disturbing its refound slumber now that it had rid itself of the grape pickers brought in for the experience of toiling from dawn until dusk amidst the vines. All that effort for the pleasure of a few *pichets* of local wine and a dormitory bed every evening as the bacchanalian bounty made its way to the rather less romantic surroundings of the wine cooperative.

The only colour that could be made out in this hungover vinescape was the occasional orange of the hunters' safety jackets as they stole from one thicket or hedgerow to another. Even the monochrome of their pick-ups parked along the road seemed to have opted for discretion so as not to warn the deer and wild boors of their imminent hunting spree.

Jacques was on his way to see his father. He had found himself in a no-woman's land. His wife was playing hard to get back, his mistress was sulking because he hadn't immediately seized on the chance to make her official and was probably looking for another way up the slippery pole of social ascension, and other women, who had seemed so plentiful when he was married, were now proving to be much more difficult to catch.

He needed male advice. His relations with his father had always been a bit complicated. Dupont senior hadn't exactly been a stable figure since his parents' divorce when he was a young boy. His presence could only be described as feline. He would be in and out of the catflap of Jacques' life according to his own whim, spending months if not years away chasing after his own existence before suddenly turning up to be fed the latest news, catch up on some rest in their house between adventures and positively straining to be fawned over as he recounted his various rocambolesque exploits.

The strange artefacts that he would bring back enthusiastically from his travels would invariably be deposited in some part of the house like a dead bird or mouse brought in to please Jacques and Catherine but that no one really wanted to touch.

A few years ago, just before his sixtieth birthday, this colourful 'Papygayo', as the children insisted on calling him, had decided that it was about time for him to set down his suitcases for a while and fallen for the doubtful charms of a rundown old chateau an hour north of his son and daughter-in-law. He fancied himself as lord of the *château* for the next part of the saga and had launched yet another hair-brained money-making scheme to give himself the life to which he intended to get accustomed.

Jacques and Catherine had called in on him a few times when he had first settled in the area, when the work on restoring the much-neglected Burgundy-stone pile had only just begun. As Jacques turned off the *Route Départémentale* and started his way up the weed-paved, plane-tree lined alley, he noticed that the scaffolding was still up and that the ivy had started to camouflage it into a modern turret. In fact, nothing much had apparently changed since his last visit.

There were still pillars missing from the stone balustrade that was sprouting grass at much the same rate as Dupont senior was losing his own tufts of hair. The once beautiful urns were bare of masterfully manicured Boxwood shrubs. Some of the windows were still patched up with cardboard and the only sign of life was the smoke coming out of one of the majestic chimneys and the battered old Diane car that was parked jauntily facing the crumbling stone steps. An old Citroen DS, as favoured by de Gaulle, gliding around the circular driveway to allow its occupants to alight graciously onto the dramatically wide steps of the entrance, would have been a more appropriate sight.

By the time Jacques had rounded the dry fountain, which served only as a leaf-play centre for the birds, the lord of the manor himself had come out onto the terrace, curious to see who was visiting him unannounced on a Sunday morning.

"*Salut* chip,"

"Chip? Since when have you called me chip papa?"

"Since you fell off the old block. Nice to see it's in the genes."

"Yes, well say that to Catherine. So you know then? Who told you?"

Jacques gave his father a quick, rather awkward, kiss on both cheeks, neither being very comfortable with the father-son dynamic.

"Oh you know, news travels. I still have some contacts back in town you know." He changed tack, "I'm going hunting. Coming with me?"

"I think we've both done enough of that and look where that's got us…" he said looking around him at the general state of disrepair.

His father gave him a sharp look.

"Yes, well these are just rich for the picking," grabbed a bucket and headed off.

For a man of his age he didn't look that bad, thought Jacques, appraising the incongruous figure as he hurried curiously behind him, equipping himself along the way with another bucket that was just lying around the gravel courtyard. His green wellies and jeans were set off by a once expensive tweed jacket under which he had on a white cotton shirt, unbuttoned low enough to show off the shark-tooth necklace he'd brought back from one of his life chapters in the French overseas territories. The white matched the stubble on his chin and head, the skin underneath perma-leathered by the elements.

"Hey *papa*, don't we need any guns or traps," he yelled as he scurried behind the decided steps of the oligarch.

In reply he only heard him yell.

"Olga!"

"Olga? Got a new dog papa?"

Dupont senior stopped in his tracks for a second as if thinking this one over then turned around.

"No, not quite as loyal I should think," he finally answered.

At this point a young, tall and strikingly blonde young woman came out languorously onto the terrace behind them and shouted back in a strongly accented Russian accent.

"Yes darling, what is it?"

Jacques was torn between admiration and jealousy.

"New acquisition?"

"Yes, Thai Mai couldn't be doing with the snails. Divinities in her country or something. Once she'd processed her way through a fair bit of my bank account she refused to start processing her way through the molluscs. Anyway, she's gone, not sure if it's back to Phuket or Pantin, but Olga doesn't seem to mind the slime."

Turning his sights back to Olga, he shouted back.

"I'm off on a hunt my little Anna Karenina. Meet my son, Jacques. Jacques meet Olga."

Olga gave a tired and indifferent little wave and turned back into the house tugging her garish silk throw around her bony shoulders. Jacques couldn't really see her cleaning, cooking and packaging snails but she definitely dolled up the château nicely.

Jacques couldn't help his next question.

"Seen *maman* lately?"

A gust of wind seemed to make the surrounding trees gasp with the boldness of the query.

The response was tinged with bitterness.

"Another one who thought she could do better without me."

"Yes, ridiculous," said Jacques ironically.

"And you?"

"Now and then when she's between St Barth and St Moritz," he answered honestly.

"And her new man?"

"Papa! It's been thirty years! No, he's too busy running The Biggest Wine Company in the World."

His father looked embarrassed that he had even asked after her and blustered on.

"Yes well, anyone can sell wine. Right, talking about business and heritage. See all this before you…"

Jacques looked up from his feet that were trying to negotiate the mud-filled furrows of the tyre tracks and looked out at the view that his father seemed eager to show him. From their raised position on the hill he could see the bag of bones of a chateau his father now called home but that were begging for a good few Michelin-standard meals to put the meat back on its emaciated skeleton. The fields around it, what could once have been manicured grounds, were in need of some national park-grade landscaping equipment but he tried hard to imagine the potential as his father continued.

"This is yours, and you have to keep onto it. You can't go and give it to the Brits. They've got most of the Dordogne and the Périgord already. Same for the kids. They were made in France weren't they? It's time for protectionism my son."

"What do you mean?"

"I heard that you've been having some fun and that she's kicked you out. You have to start looking after your interests, although thinking about *numero uno* was probably what got you into this mess in the first place. Don't worry. I know all about it."

At this point he got down on his knees along a stone wall and started rummaging around, apparently chasing the snails.

"Get some dirt on her. Turn it around. Don't be done for fault. I'll help you. I'll pay for the best lawyers."

Jacques raised a doubtful eyebrow at that point but continued to listen to the wisdom of age.

"Just follow my lead," he said, at which point Dupont Senior slid in the mud and fell flat onto his face.

"Damn, that one got away."

Jacques was quite taken aback by this vehemence against his wife. He realised that everything he had done, the spying, the following, the creeping, the stalking had been done to date to try to get her back, because he was jealous of anyone else having her, touching her, spending time in her company, enjoying the privilege of making love to her.

"So I let her go?"

His father was standing up by now with a scattering of snails in his bucket and his entire front soiled by his efforts.

"Do you still see Her?" he asked

Jacques wasn't sure who he was talking about.

"Who?" Then it clicked, "Ah, HER? To be honest she kind of put the iron curtain back up when I told her that west was finally best."

By now they were back in the vicinity of the chateau and his father's completely irony-free "Send her to me whenever you want" fell on Olga's youthful ears as she was making her way from the main house to some outbuilding, by now wearing very short shorts and wellington boots as if she was on the way to an English music festival. She swore at him in Russian and tore the buckets from them with their meagre takings and marched off with them into the nerve centre of Dupont Senior's snail farming empire.

Dupont senior just sighed as he looked at the sight of Olga's derrière striding away. "Well maybe you should have a last try at winning back the missus then. Take her back where you first met. Organise a summit meeting, hammer it out…" he said, leering rather creepily for a paternal conversation.

Jacques was weighing up what he said.

"You may have something there. Relight the fire and all that. I can't have her taking me to the cleaners. I don't know if she would, she has enough resources of her own. But you never know. So you'll take the children for the weekend?"

Dupont senior hadn't seen that one coming but supposed that he should try out his unpractised role as grandfather once in a while.

"Don't know about that. I'll see with Olga if she does pampers as well as champers."

Jacques couldn't help his snide comment, spurred on as much by jealousy as anything else.

"Well she is closer to their age than to yours. It'll give them a Barbie to play with. Maybe it's time you tried your hand at being a parent."

Without waiting for a reaction he started walking towards his car.

"*Au revoir papa.* I have to go. I have tickets to book. See you sometime."

His father just gave him a wistful wave, concern briefly crossing his already sun-scarred face. He liked Catherine despite his earlier warnings. Though he may never have told him, he'd admired his son for landing such a great woman, for making such lovely children, doing what he'd never managed to do, settle down, buy a nice house, keep down a good job. They'd seemed happy whenever he'd popped in between planes. Why had he gambled all of that away?

After searching all his life he'd never really come close to contentment. He'd obviously passed his affliction onto his son. What he really wanted to tell him was that nothing could beat what he already had. That he had already had it all.

Suddenly tired, he turned his thoughts back to his own trials and tribulations and made his way to the outhouse to get back into Olga's good books by getting into somewhere else. God, he was starting to get too old for this game.

CHAPTER 27

Six months into the separation and life was following its new course. It wasn't one that Catherine had chosen but the storm seemed to have sent her down another disused river bed. Disused and bed seemed very apt she thought to herself as she stepped out of the house one morning to get the post. She had to admit the loneliness was getting to her, especially that late-night solitude when the children were asleep and she was alone with herself, her own thoughts, her own choices.

The pain of the treason had turned into a numb vacuum. Cold water had been thrown over the frantic ardour of Jacques' clumsy attempts at stalking and intimidation, and on the dating games organised by her friends for that matter. She couldn't claim to be happy or content but there was a kind of normality in her non-sensical situation.

She seemed to have two choices at this point. Let herself be carried down this new course and see where it would take her or try to paddle her way back upstream to the confluence and try to join the main river again.

The more she thought about it however, mainstream had never been her thing. She'd never really gone with the flow. She'd jumped over one Channel, chosen a profession where she had no boss, no one telling her what to do or when to do it, she'd traced her own route, followed her gut feeling until now, headed off as her heart took her.

What was one more branch in the river for her? Nothing, except that this time she seemed to be down the creek without a paddle.

Catherine had come back from the school run and was getting ready to settle down to write for the day. She had just popped back to get the post so that she wouldn't be tempted to use it as an excuse to stop working.

She opened the post box and took out its contents of junk mail and bills and an intriguing envelope marked only with her name. There was no mystery surrounding the hand though. It was the same that had signed their wedding register 13 years ago.

She opened it as she walked back to the house, pulling out papers that she presumed were divorce or money-related.

She was rather confused when she saw the flight tickets. They had her name on them. She was apparently booked for a weekend in Berlin before Christmas. She had stopped in her tracks and only the biting December wind propelled her back into the house.

Once back in front of the warmth of the log fire she'd got going that morning so that she could write in front of it instead of freezing in the cold office, she shook all the contents of the brown envelope out onto the glass coffee table.

A note floated out. She hesitated before reading it, knowing that it would face her with a quandary. Why was he doing this? The scab was healing. Why pick at it and have to deal with all the bloody mess inside again?

She poured out some coffee from the Bodum coffee maker into her oversized mug, gulped a bit down and then started reading.

"*Ma chère* Catherine. Do you remember our first meeting in Berlin? I kissed you under the Brandenburg gate. We got drunk together on Erdinger in the Biergartens of Tiergarten. We went to Techno clubs in former bunkers with Graffiti-covered walls dripping with the condensed sweat of hundreds of dancers, we ate *Currywurst* on Wittenbergplatz and did Berlin by night on the N 1 *Nachtbus*. I want to take you back to your future. See you at the airport. *Je t'ai aimé. Je t'aime et je t'aimerai.*"

Catherine couldn't help but be annoyed by his grammatical word games and her first thought was that it was all very well to have loved her in the past, to love her in the present and even promise to love her in the future, but maybe if "*il l'avait aimé plus*", had he loved her more, then things wouldn't have been as tense in the first place.

As far as love declarations went it wasn't a bad move but she didn't know what to think. Yes, they'd had good times then but were they the same people now? Wasn't it a dangerous game trying to relive the past?

If she was honest she had hated techno music then and still hated it now. It was just so intricately linked to that time and that place that she had gone along with the intense feet-gazing and sudden arm-pointing in smiley t-shirts. The same went for the bus journey home. What he had forgotten to mention was that it had usually entailed waiting for the damned thing for half an hour in minus twenty degree temperatures and then walking back to their student digs from the end of the line that felt one stop short of Siberia. She'd also long since swapped Currywurst for sushi and beer for Burgundy. As for the dripping with sweat bit, the only place she wanted to do that these days was in a steam room followed by a vigorous black soap exfoliation session in some Hammam in Marrakesh.

She was afraid that going with him down memory lane would just remind her why they had drifted apart, that one of them had changed and the other hadn't.

Of course, it could also remind her of why she had fallen in love with him in the first place. And it would be the best Christmas gift she could give her children. A bauble of hope on the Christmas tree that they had put up half-heartedly this year, knowing that their family wouldn't be together for the celebrations. The question was whether it was what she actually wanted from Santa this year? Did she want to be a gift in his stocking or just sock it to him?

She tried to put her focus back on her writing but her concentration was gone. She turned over the piece of paper and saw Jacques' explanation that his father and his girlfriend Olga would be happy to look after the children for the weekend. She lifted a bemused eyebrow at that thought. It wasn't really an argument that swung the pendulum in his favour. While she had thought her father-in-law a bit of a laugh, quite liking his unconventional take on life, she had visions of him more as a hell–raiser than a child-raiser, and as for Olga, well somehow she doubted that he'd hooked up with Mary Poppins.

It was mid-December. She still had time to think about. He wasn't asking for an answer. Just for her presence at a certain time and place. So why did it feel like a date with history?

***

For the next two weeks, Catherine's life was spent wondering whether the invitation she had received on that First Day of Christmas was really from her "true love" or whether he could keep his "turtle doves" of peace, his "French hens" and "gold rings" because this maid was not for milking.

Between the present hunting and packing and Christmas market-going with the children she wore Romain down with her incessant advice-seeking, but on the eve of the trip she still had no idea whether she should stay or go.

By 7 p.m. she had fetched the weekend case from the attic but it was left unopened in the middle of her dressing room like a Samsonite tombstone.

By 8 p.m. she'd found her passport at the bottom of her summer handbag, abandoned in the back of the cupboard since her last trip home, but she simply put it down visibly on the desk in the office like some kind of post-it to remind her of the trip.

The children were with her husband for the start of the Christmas holiday so she had no excuse at the ready to get out of it. He had taken care of that and she couldn't come up with any last-minute children's illness that could give her an easy way out of her easy jet flight.

By 9 p.m. she had worked herself into a state and through most of a bottle of red wine. Her gut feeling told her not to go, that he had hurt her too much, that he had killed the love that she had once felt for him, that his betrayal couldn't be forgotten with a weekend getaway.

The truth was that she didn't miss him that much.

The mistress had only been the white-blonde tip of the iceberg. Below the surface, they had been tempting a Titanicesque disaster for a long time. They had hidden the problems from the world, they had padded out the void with possessions, homes, furnishings and an apparently glamorous lifestyle. But it was now clear to her that it was all a glossy wall of impenetrable ice that was transparent in its emptiness, that had clearly evaporated upon contact with a warm body and that her dragon's fire had melted into nothingness in one fell swoop back on that balmy June night.

She took another slug of wine. The faces then started swimming in front of her eyes, the collateral victims of the shipwreck of her marriage. Manon and Arthur were reaching out for her, crying "Do it for us", her mother was gasping at her to "Save the family home", her friends weaving between them, enjoining her not to break the social circle that she had built around her. "Go on! Come back into the net."

She drowned in her own tears, submerged by her saline streams of sorrow and wept herself to sleep, a sleep tormented by these ghosts of Christmas past.

CHAPTER 28

It was like standing at the altar, waiting for the bride to arrive in the limousine, thought Jacques as he hovered before the check-in desk. The colourful scarf tied jauntily around the airline staff's neck was one up on a vicar's monochromatic dog collar, but both had similar powers to send them off to marital heaven. All that Jacques needed now was for his potential ex-wife-to-be to turn up and say yes I do want an aisle seat.

By now he was being overtaken by a whole pack of cabin cases, which meant that he would probably be the one asked to put his in the hold. He shuffled backwards to let the other passengers pass and looked at his watch, again. There were only 10 minutes until they closed check-in for their flight. But there was no way that she would give up on this chance. He knew that she didn't have the children this weekend. This was him offering himself to her on a plate, saying sorry in style. *Merde*, not turning up would just be rude.

He took another glance at his watch, checking it against the minimalist clock taking up the entire wall opposite him. With each forward lurch of the man-size minute hand he felt himself being pushed towards the hour and he felt that it was sending him a message. There would be a before and an after that deadline, whatever happened.

He caught one of the bescarved girls' eye, shrugged and opened his eyes wide to convey his helplessness and to earn her sympathy in case she refused to let them board. He looked back towards the rotating doors further down the hallway.

***

At the same time, Catherine was just sitting there with the engine running. It wasn't a further attempt to end her life with a car that, this time, wasn't electric but an attempt to make sense of her life with a taxi driver as an improvised therapist.

"Look *madame*," Janno was saying, "we can sit here all day *si vous voulez*, I don't care, my motor is running and the meter is turning. But if you want to take that flight, you'd better decide whether you love the *salaud* or not. Or just go for the free holiday. Think of it as one of those timeshare schemes where they pay for your holiday as long as you visit their show apartment and sit through the sales blurb. But there's no obligation to buy at the end however much they try to pressure you into it."

"But that wouldn't be fair to him," protested Catherine. "I don't want to lead him on."

"Madame, I can see how you got into this situation, you're just too *gentille*, too nice, you have to be one of those *femmes fatales* who use and abuse. Stop trying to please everyone else and think about yourself for once."

They'd been parked in front of the terminal with the engine running like a getaway car for the best part of half an hour by then, except that she was the coveted heist and didn't really want to share it with her Clyde. She couldn't do it. She knew she couldn't but she also knew that as soon as she told Janno to step on it there was no turning back this time, that Bonnie would be going it alone.

So she just sat there until time caught up with the point of no return and took the decision for her.

***

At the stroke of midday, the hostesses called for any remaining passengers to check-in for the Berlin flight.

At 12:01, passengers were confused to see a taxi speeding away from the terminal, tyres screeching. Usually that's how passengers reached the airport when they were late for their flight. In the other direction it looked rather suspicious. They also wondered at the seasonal snow shower that seemed to be streaming from the back window until they picked up the shredded pieces and saw that they were a plane ticket that would never be exchanged for a boarding pass.

At 12:02, a lone male was the last passenger to be hurriedly registered for the 12:40 flight to Berlin. Yes, he would be travelling alone. No, *madame* would not be joining him. Did he mind having his cabin bag put in the hold because the flight was full? Yes, but he guessed he had no choice.

"No," said the face above the duty scarf, "it's a bit late now. You should have thought about it sooner."

***

In the taxi, Janno was thinking about the story he had to tell his *potes* at the corner bar tonight and the fare he would make doing the return journey for this *folle* plus the waiting time.

On the back seat, Catherine was on the phone.

"Hey Anne, you know the ski apartment you were telling me about? Is it still free this week? Yes, change of plan. I'll be taking the children."

***

At the same time Jacques was being manhandled through the airport security checks after the handcuffs he'd brought along in case he needed to spice up his kiss-and-make-up session with Catherine brought the entire security team running and at the same time brought rather broad smiles to his fellow-travellers' faces. He was then named and shamed as being the late passenger holding up the flight and had to find his mid-plane window seat to some very nasty stares from everyone on the aircraft.

The empty seat beside him, the only one on the plane, taunted him for the next hour and a half, a constant reminder that he had been jilted at the counter.

She hadn't signed the truce, which meant that this was war. Not the silly little war games they'd been playing out to date but full-blown warfare. He would bring in the allies and launch hostilities as soon as he landed and emerged from this forced cease-fire.

By then he had downed a few rationed bottles of Syrah and decided that his blueprint for war would begin after having looked up the old gang and eventually an old girlfriend in Berlin and catching up over a few beers.

Managing to capture a hostess in the conveniently empty seat beside him for a few minutes, he decided that his army basic training for the onslaught ahead was successful. It was *décidemment* better than 'Get the Boot Camp' at least.

CHAPTER 29

Picking up the children from Château Dupont had been quite an experience for Catherine. It had been the first time she had come face to face with her ex-father in law since the separation. She'd greeted him cordially. He had performed the double cheeked kiss with his customary relish but had refrained this time from mischievously pinching her bum, a sure sign that she was no longer family.

After the initial surprise and, she sensed, a twinge of dismay triggered by her sudden arrival, there was a distinct sense of relief in the air when she announced that she was taking the children away for a hastily-arranged skiing holiday. Dupont senior looked as listless as his snails after only a few hours in the children's company, and, to go by the shop-bought packs of *croque-monsieur* cheese and ham toasties piled up in the kitchen, Olga's only culinary skills consisted of spooning black blobs of caviar into her mouth between gulps of Dom Perignon.

Arthur hugged her for saving him from a night of terror, having already started to conjure up images in his head of the monster-sized molluscs under his bed. Manon was the only one who seemed disappointed that her weekend trying on the erotic content of Olga's walk-in wardrobe had been cut short. In fairy tale terms, given the overriding absence of fabric, she'd been playing make believe with the Emperor's New Clothes rather than Cinderella's ball gown but the Ali Baba's cavern of silk and sequins that had kept Manon entertained since her arrival now meant that she wanted to be Olga when she grew up.

Catherine heard all about Papygayo's castle and Olga's burnt pasta lunch as they drove up towards the ski retreat Anne had lent them at the last minute. Anne herself was hosting Christmas in the city for her family who had flown there from the States for the holiday and wasn't heading for the hills until New Year's Eve and was only too happy to let Catherine and the children use it as a hideaway lest Jacques decide to follow them. Catherine had no idea whether he had gone to Berlin without her or not. For all she knew he could be walking down Unter den Linden or knocking at her door in St Desirée as she made her escape.

Wherever he was, it was better to give him time to cool down in case she had added insult to injury with her no-show at the airport.

As they came around the last of the hairpin bends they had been slowly negotiating up the mountain, all her concerns fell by the wayside to join the mud-speckled icy sludge.

The Alpine tableau that welcomed them seemed backlit by the pink sun setting behind rather phallic granite peaks with their frosted toppings. Catherine shook off the thought and drove through the forest of wooden chalets, past the quaint restaurants with their promises of *tartiflette* and *fondu Savoyard* and on to the outskirts of the village towards the address Anne had given her over the phone.

Even in the impending darkness, the chalet exuded charm and warmth and, as she parked in front of it, Catherine sensed that she had made the right choice, that this was where she was supposed to be and that this haven, hundreds of metres above sea level, offered a good vantage point to take stock of her life.

She was pulled from her thoughts by the snowball the children had thrown at her windscreen. She jumped out of the car to get her revenge and they spent the next five minutes in a frenzied snowball fight before the ethereal flakes turned to icy water as it melted into the coats and formed heavy icicles in their hair.

They warmed up by hauling the bags, skis, boots and helmets up the two stone steps and into the log-cabin's minimalist chic interior with its white and beige colour scheme, fur throws and cowhide mats. The kitchen with its sleek modern appliances discretely encased in reclaimed wood and the large chrome hood to niftily extract all lingering hints of *raclette* odours glowed in the dimmed lights. Logs were already artfully arranged in the circular stone hearth that took up the centre of the open-plan living area and colourful politically-correct sculptures of hunting trophies replaced the traditionally mounted heads with their glazed eyes and smell of death and formaldehyde.

As soon as everything was brought in from the car, the children rushed off to choose their beds while Catherine flopped onto the contemporary chaise-longue by the window and looked out over the flickering stream of light formed by the torch-bearing ski instructors on the nearby slope as they entertained the tourists with their nocturnal descents.

She couldn't wait to be out there herself, but in the meantime she had beds to make up, wet clothes to dry, hungry children to feed, and, last but not least, skiing lessons to book online for the kids and beginner's snowboarding for herself. It was time to try something different.

CHAPTER 30

Perfect conditions for blue-sky thinking, Catherine said to herself as she strode out of the chalet and straight into the fresh mound of snow that had carpeted the stone steps. She breathed in the icy fresh air and felt it already starting to kill the germs that had made her sick to the stomach over the past six months. She closed her eyes and took in another gulp, and then yet another of this free drug prescribed by nature to ward away the winter blues.

Invigorated, she helped the children put on their skis and gave them a push start down the short driveway. Her spirits held up even as she pulled them with their poles through the resort to the meeting point for their skiing lessons. Seasoned skiers already, Arthur was doing his 3rd Star and Manon was already on her Bronze.

She rubbed Manon's hands to keep them warm as they waited in the winter wonderland, told her son off for rolling about in the snow and getting his socks wet but, before long, they were off in their colourful ski-school bibs, pushing hard on their poles to keep up with the teacher effortlessly skating up the slope towards the ski lifts along with the other groups. The overall effect was that of an excursion organised by a Pied Piper convention.

Wishing she had time for a hot chocolate but already late for her "Discovery" level snowboard lesson, Catherine weaved her way through the anxious parents, howling toddlers and red-clad ski instructors with their tell-tale white rimmed eyes in Toblerone-brown faces. The meeting point was at the Ski School office, where she was to team up with her teacher for the week, Jean-Baptiste.

Until now, she had always turned up her nose at snow-boarding. The funkily dressed youngsters in their crazy and colourful woolly hats had always annoyed her with their ice-scraping rear approaches, tendency to change direction without warning and habit of sitting right in the middle of the ski run, forcing you to deviate from the route you had carefully plotted further up the mountain.

She just hoped that the teacher wasn't one of these young hipsters who would much rather be sharing a joint with a twenty something up on a rocky outcrop than sharing tips with an almost forty-something on the best way to balance on an ironing board.

Going into the ski school to be matched with a teacher was a bit like going into a bar when you had a blind date. She couldn't help but eye up all the instructors, liking the look of some but crossing her fingers that some of the older ones, weathered by the mountains but still under the impression that the *Ecole de Ski Française* badge gave them the same mythical irresistibility as a pilot's uniform, would be dispatched off to shepherd the *Piou Pious* and the *Oursons* around the nursery slopes.

A woman instructor would be perfect, she thought, as she saw a kind-looking, Heidi-plaited Savoyard redcoat having a laugh with a colleague, whose back was turned towards her. But Jean-Baptiste was hardly a girl's name in France, unless she'd misread it and she was actually a Jeanne, the two last letters operating a semiotic sex change. She was snapped out of her musings about whether the teacher could actually be a Scottish Jean, a heroic Joan or even a misspelt Spanish

Juan when she heard the receptionist call her name and that of her allocated teacher.

Expectantly, Catherine waited for one of the pack of instructors to come forward like the selected contestant on a dating show. The receptionist called again and the chosen one tore himself away from his laugh-riddled conversation with the plait lady and made his way towards the counter.

He was definitely a Jean, a French John, pronounced as if the 'n' that usually brought the name to a neat and definitive conclusion had been forgotten and exchanged for a panting gasp at the end. It was a name filled with the promise left by the open-mouthed 'o'.

He was probably about 35, Catherine guessed, which closed the age gap if not the experience gap. He didn't have the ubiquitous goatee beard but had a two-day stubble that gave him a rugged outdoor look and a certain masculinity to his pretty features. His eyes were a light blue and when he smiled across at her the laughter lines creased up, hiding the white bands that betrayed either his good natured temperament or habit of squinting up at the sun.

She was still taking him in when he extended his hand and asked her if she was the "Catherine" he had the privilege of spending the morning with. He probably used the line every day on every female customer over fifteen so Catherine gave him a polite smile and hoped that he didn't notice her heart skip a beat when he took her gloved hand in his.

She spent the next two hours mostly standing still on her immobile board trying to find her balance, giving the odd hoola-hooping hip movement to get it moving and then falling down onto her bruised and abused derriere, where she would stay until Jean-Baptiste pulled her up with a good-humoured tug to start the whole process again.

She felt clumsy, heavy and out of the loop as she saw others swerve their way past them with only minimal bodily contortions and was about to tell Jean-Baptiste that she should probably stick with traditional skiing when he positioned himself behind her.

"I don't usually start with this technique on the first day, I like to get to know my students better first, but I want to show you how much fun snowboarding is before you give up."

Catherine could hardly answer as this last appeal had been made right into her ear, or at least as close to it as he could get through her helmet, while Jean-Baptiste's hands were busy repositioning her legs and hips and correcting her stance. By the time he reached her shoulders, she was positively shivering with excitement.

She had no idea what was coming over her. It seemed as if her entire body was coming alive again, awakening from a deep hibernation she had thrown herself into back in July. But like a bear waking from his deep sleep before winter was out, she was dazed and confused and rather hungry now that she had been prematurely aroused from her slumber.

She tried to tell herself that the tingling sensations on her skin were in fact frostbite but when Jean-Baptiste pushed his groin into her padded ski trousers to push them down the hill together, she gave up the lie and started to enjoy the thaw that seemed to be setting in all over her body. Yes, it was definitely time to try something new.

CHAPTER 31

Early next morning, fresh as an edelweiss after a muscle-soothing bath and a good night's sleep in luxury linen, Catherine was hogging the bathroom mirror before having to make sure the children had a good breakfast down them and packing them into their skiing clobber.

Her usual ski holiday ritual was a layer of tinted high-factor sun cream and a quickly pulled ponytail between the croissant run and the black run. Putting on any eye make-up was just tempting a disastrous face-down plunge into a semi-concealed stream on the side of the *piste* and the resulting ravages. Today, she decided that the time had come to perfect her winter sports style and to join the ranks of those who managed to pull off the ice queen look.

She worked her hair into a long thick braid to keep her hair out of her face, not that she was doing much more than a kilometre an hour on her snowboard for the time being, and applied her make-up with today's après-ski in mind. She felt those forgotten stirrings in her lower stomach again just the thought of the 'date'.

After yesterday's lesson, Jean-Baptiste had suggested going for a pre-lunch drink to celebrate her "baptism of fire with Baptiste" as he put it. Cringing at his well-worn joke but secretly flattered that he had asked her at all, she had declined as she had to pick up the children but promised to join him another day. He was just being friendly, she told herself, but she knew very well that there was no such thing as a free après-ski.

Manon's voice outside the door telling her that Arthur had stolen her ski socks brought her round to more urgent concerns and the clunking, clomping and clonking of ski equipment and accessories noisily filled the next hour until she found herself back on the pristinely ploughed slopes with J-B, as he preferred to be called.

An hour into the lesson and Catherine was trying with all her might to concentrate on her turning and carving but knew that she was a long way from performing any tricks any time soon. On a snowboard at least. J-B hadn't said anything about the post-lesson drink and she was starting to think that the invitation had been a figment of her imagination. But a quarter of an hour before the lesson was up he put his hands on her shoulders, just to steady her, she imagined and said, "Why don't we go over the theory over a drink. A friend of mine has a bar just here on the *piste.*"

Catherine accepted with pleasure this time, confident in the knowledge that, when she took off her helmet, the braid would have kept her hair from doing the static Mexican wave. Vain maybe but, as she told herself, controlling your mane was the first step towards getting back into the saddle.

The electro-soul vibe of the lunchtime DJs welcomed them as they boarded towards the bar. J-B pulled up at the wooden ski-racks with flair in a flurry of fresh snow. Catherine hadn't quite mastered stopping yet and just ended up on her back in a flustered flurry of embarrassment. J-B gave her his hand and pulled her up so hard that she almost toppled him over. They ended up sunglasses to sunglasses, separated only by the thickness of their lip balm.

"I'd better get us a few beers to cool us down," he said with his ice-melting smile.

Catherine took her hand away from his steadying chest, smiled with embarrassment, told him that she'd look for a couple of loungers out on the terrace and did her best to walk seductively up the wooden steps in her snowboarding shoes, suddenly realising that stilettos really were a girl's best friend and that hoping that your bum didn't look big was a futile exercise when you were wearing ski pants.

She found two loungers together and bagged them, turning them strategically away from the two Moncler-clad twenty-somethings beside them sipping champagne between blasé drags on their cigarettes. This was the first "proper" date she'd had in twenty years. She had to put all the chances on her side. The view over the Alps was straight out of a brochure and, while for J-B it may have been just another day at the office, she still wanted to make sure he enjoyed his break at the "coffee machine".

She saw him on his way back, joking with the waiters and waving at familiar faces. There was no doubt about it. He really was charming. God more than that, he captured all the thrills and spills of the mountains. There and then she decided that she wouldn't say no to any extra lessons he had to offer.

By the end of the first beer the conversation had turned from snowboarding to their off-piste lives. By the time the second had washed down the first, she had filled him in on her separation and he was patting her thigh in commiseration. Even through her thermals she could feel the hot tingle. By the end of the third, she had agreed to go clubbing with him that night once the children were in bed.

Heading down the slopes light-headedly to fetch the children from their lesson, she knew that the exhilaration wasn't just down to her sudden, Dutch-courage driven mastery of the blue run. She felt alive, but that feeling of alive you get only when you're on the edge. The question was how deep was the crevice below and was she ready to tackle such a perilous run. She stopped to catch her breath and decided that it would be a good time to get some advice before she ended up with a broken something, definitely not heart, but trust maybe, especially in her own judgement.

She took out her phone, miraculously found that she had a network connection and waited for Flo to answer. She was relieved to hear her unmistakable Catherine Deneuve-accented voice answer her from Gstaad, where, to go by the sound of crystal, lunch wasn't a home-made sandwich and cereal bar on a chairlift or an over-priced Frankfurter and *frites* and the house red in a self-service restaurant full of screaming children and sunburnt Northern Europeans.

"Flo it's me, well I think it's me, but it could be someone else, someone else who is thinking of ..." lowering her voice as a couple of skiers passed her "... doing it with a ski instructor. What do you think? Too clichéd, too much of a stereotype, too early?"

Flo gave a little screech before Catherine heard her ordering more champagne from a passing waiter.

"It's perfect darling. Just what you need. Just think of him as the plumber who's going to unblock the pipes to get you back into the flow. I'll be thinking of you darling."

"I'd rather you didn't. I don't even want to think about it myself. I can't even believe that he fancies me."

Catherine heard a sigh on the other side of the line.

"I'm not going to lie to you *ma cocotte*, he probably just fancies his chances. But you know what they say, a ski instructor is not for life, just for the season. Call me with the details once you get your ski pass darling. And enjoy. *Ciao bella*."

CHAPTER 32

Anna's chalet really did come with everything, "all mum cons" in fact, including a baby sitter's number on the fridge door. Catherine took the fact that she was available at such short notice as a sign of destiny and used the children's nap time to give her body a short-notice spa session in the chalet's opulent master bathroom.

She tried to concentrate on the practicalities, knowing that if she gave too much leeway to her emotions or listened to reason a cheese *fondu* would be the only thing bubbling and squeaking tonight. But she was as nervous as a novice, and preen and prune as she may on the outside, her insides were a knot of fear and dread intertwined with a writhing branch strewn with the sharp thorns of desire.

She had dinner with the children before putting them to bed with a film and instructions to be good for the babysitter. She had been tempted all evening to phone J –B and call the whole thing off but his text message saying how much he looked forward to discovering what lay beneath the ski clothes propelled her back to the bedroom. She hastily changed from her faithful jeans into a suede mini skirt that she teamed with knee-high boots to make it through the snow and a fringed tunic cut low enough to make him want to take the beaded tassels and pull her to him for some warmth. Or so she was really starting to hope.

Catherine shivered in her quilted jacket as she made her way through the snow-carpeted village streets. The post-skiing drinkers still in their thermals were hanging out of the bars and the pre-

Christmas revellers, already gorged with mountain cheeses, forest mushrooms and Alpine pasta and polenta, were schlepping their way home towards a digestive tipple of *génépi*, with its pungent bouquet of alpine meadows that left you anything but fresh and floral the morning after.

Catherine looked up at the behind-the-scenes ballet of the ploughs, snowscaping the churned powder on the slopes into a Japanese zen garden to be vandalised again tomorrow into a confused squiggle of lines and shapes by the tagging skis and boards.

Lost in her thoughts, a car, top heavy with its thick helmet of snow, narrowly missed her as it skidded in all directions and she felt herself fall backwards over the camouflaged pavement in her attempt to step backwards to avoid it.

For the second time that day, a pair of strong hands caught her before she touched the ground.

"It's a good thing that I'm around," said J-B's familiar voice as he turned her around to face him and gently pushed her dishevelled hair from her eyes. "You don't need a ski instructor; you need a bodyguard."

That was it. She was Whitney Houston. He made it all so easy, it was like being in a film. It was as if the lines were already written, as if a director was out there somewhere dictating the action, telling them how to move, showing her how to respond, putting the words in their mouth and taking the scene to its pre-drafted climax.

"I think it would be rude not to reward you," she heard herself saying and feeling distinctively May West-like she gently brushed his lips with hers, in gratitude.

She must have expressed more than that though as, after she pulled back he looked with a bemused inquiry into her eyes as if to check her intentions, before responding with a kiss that betrayed not only his long experience as a ski instructor, but also his nationality.

"Why don't we skip the club," he said, coming up for air.

Given her last experience at a night club, Catherine thought this was the best offer she'd had in a long time. She nodded her agreement. He put her hand in hers and pulled her along the slippery streets. She was feeling like a Disney princess on ice. Who would have ever thought that skates were optional? She was gliding and spinning as it was and just in the mood for figure skating.

She hesitated only on the way into J-B's bachelor pad above a ski hire shop and turned around on a hunch just to check that no one was watching her, not that she knew anyone in the resort. She heard the dead thud and puff of falling snow but presumed it was just a slab coming off a roof somewhere nearby.

She quickly turned back to matters at hand and closed the door on the outside world and on a chapter in her life. She wasn't opening a new one, she was keeping that for another time and place. No, this was just the divide between the chapters, the binding in her attempt to keep her life together.

She went into the apartment and turned down the sheets to mark the place from where to pick up her life again in a few hours' time.

CHAPTER 33

"*Maman*, hey *maman*, we do have a flight to catch you know. We can't miss Christmas in Wales with grandma," Manon reminded her as Catherine stood by the cases waiting to be loaded into her 4x4 with a dopey smile on her face.

But it was Arthur half bumping, half sliding down the steps on his ride-on suitcase that jerked her out of her daydreams of the night before.

"It will burst open if you do that and your little pants will be everywhere," she teased him before picking it up and pushing it into the last space left in the boot.

"Right, everybody in, we're off," she said, recklessly taking the steps two at a time with her refound energy to go and close up her friend's heaven-sent haven. She took a last look around the rooms, saved a forgotten *doudou* from under a bed where it had no one to comfort, righted the cowhide carpet and locked the door behind her with a sigh.

It had been Berlin or bust. It had definitely been bust. If she hadn't known it when she screeched away from the airport the other day, she knew it now. The night before had been perfect. Not in any love of her life, arrows through hearts, they all lived happy ever after kind of way. But, as Florence had so aptly put it, she was back in the flow. She was Catherine unplugged.

She jumped into the car and put on the radio loudly to get them into the mood for the rocking, rolling trip down the winding roads.

"Say goodbye to the mountains," she told the kids as they passed the ski school and the lunchtime crowd taking their places at the sun-drenched terraces. Suddenly she saw him, unmistakeable even in his red uniform. His smile more pristine than the snow, his eyes bluer than the cloud-free sky. He was standing behind another woman, similar in age and looks to her, his hand in the now familiar pose within decency distance of her hips, his groin within groaning distance of her bottom.

"Well you're a fast worker aren't you," she muttered, but with a knowing smile on her face.

Arthur already had his earphones half way on, ready to lose himself in his ipad.

"What are you talking about mum?"

"Oh nothing, it's just the ski instructor who took me off piste this week darling."

"Oh, was it good?"

"Mm, yes quite exciting actually. I'll probably find the other runs easier now."

But he was gone into another world of clans and virtual clashes,

"Yeah, great mum."

She headed back down into the valleys from the gleaming heights, not sure where the road would take her but knowing that her road trip would always be better than the dead-end she had faced before.

CHAPTER 34

Catherine's bottom was taking up the entire screen, wiggling provocatively up at them, before it was covered by another one that came up from behind, clearly a man. There she could be seen again, spluttering the white stuff from her mouth, clearly finding the whole thing very amusing.

From another angle, she could be seen grabbing onto the man's chest and heaving herself up suggestively, clearly throwing herself at the poor guy. Her hand lingered just a fraction too long on his arm as she tried to get herself into position for another go.

Jacques was sickened by what he was seeing on the laptop in front of him. His wife throwing away the chance of a weekend away with him to throw herself at another man in the snow in this way.

The Gopro was now hurtling down a black run, quickly passing Catherine and the instructor who were clearly fondling each other every chance they had. It was like something out of a Red Bull extreme sport competition, except that the competitor was clearly out of his depth and the film came to an abrupt stop as the camera, or rather its wearer, plunged helmet first into the drifts on the side of the slope. The next part, the two lovebirds sitting together having a beer on a sunny terrace, had to be watched between the droplets still streaming down the lens, which gradually appeared to freeze into fuzzy icicles, giving the scene a romantically filtered feel.

The expletives hadn't stopped coming out of Jacques' mouth since he started looking at his father's film. As soon as he had arrived in

Berlin he had given his dad a call, asked him if he could take some time-out from snail farming and told him to follow Catherine the moment she turned up to fetch the children.

Always one for an adventure, his father had jumped at the chance to play at being a spy and to leave his Russian Bond girl for a few days. The honeymoon period was over and she was turning into Dr No whenever he tried to charm those sexy Wellington boots off her.

As he tracked Catherine and the children all the way to what she thought of as her safe house in the Alps, Dupont Senior had felt young again. It had brought back memories of his youth, those good old days of keeping out of the sight of jealous husbands and covering his steps because of his own irate wife. He had checked into the closest available hotel, with a view from the balcony over the very classy chalet she seemed to have rented – another detail to mention to his son –and had spent the next few days in his rather outdated skiwear, having favoured more clement climes in the past few years, trying to remaster the art of skiing while taking a crash course in the dolly shot.

The film had spluttered to a rather messy ending. The last thing they had seen was Catherine going into the ski instructor's building. She seemed to look directly at the camera as it was noiselessly camouflaged in what appeared to be the remnants of a cheese fondu.

"Couldn't you find another place to hide papa? I mean, a bin? I told you that I would pay for the camera but do you know how much those things cost?!"

"Yes well, next time you want to play candid camera, get Tarantino to do it," his father muttered before getting back to the whole point of the filming. "So what are you going to do now? You've got the proof. She's not flying back into your arms and not signing up for any convents. I'd fancy my chances as well if she wasn't your ex."

"*Mais* Papa! That's just … *putain* it's almost incestuous!"

"I just think that you're the one who's going to be taking the vow of celibacy. I can almost see the bald patch growing on your scalp as we speak."

Jacques looked pointedly at his father's brush-over hair style and raised a sarcastic eyebrow.

"So much for parental support. I've just watched my wife on film behaving like a snow hussy with another man and that's what I get."

"Look, if you want support, do what I do."

At that, he gave a quick look over his shoulder to check that his very own KGB agent wasn't around meeting her domestic security brief and went into counter-intelligence mode by typing a website address into the computer before turning it round for his son to see.

"'French Flirt'?" What the hell's that?"

"I'm telling you son, if we'd had that when I was younger, I would never have got married in the first place. I would have just gone around the world in eighty…"

Jacques put his hand over his father's mouth. Having a lecherous old fool for a progenitor wasn't easy and he could imagine why his well-born mother had quickly thrown him out. Papa had been trying and failing miserably to find the same rare diamond since. All he'd managed to unearth were fake stones and rough crystals.

"Just don't say it papa. Are you honestly suggesting that I try internet dating? *Maman* sent me to rallies to find the right girl, I went to dance lessons, for God's sake, I can deshell a prawn with a knife and fork while keeping up a conversation on the birth of the Fifth Republic on my left and Stendhal's *Le Rouge et le Noir* on my right. I didn't do all that to end up with a trowelfull of desperate divorcees."

His father looked at him with pity, as if he hadn't quite realised the wealth this mine had to offer.

"One word *mon fils*. Olga."

At that point the young woman herself passed through the living room wearing only the flimsiest silk teddy under an exotic black kimono that trailed behind her in the gust of lust that her appearance had unleashed. Both men looked on as her long, white-blond hair caressed her shoulders and lower back, and as her withering look had the very reverse effect on their own bodily functions.

As soon as the vision had disappeared up the majestic stairway, showing her toned, neck-crushing legs with every step, Jacques grabbed the computer and started filling in the form on the screen.

After all, a little prospection never hurt anyone.

CHAPTER 35

Blissfully unaware that she had been a subject of a covert operation by the divorce police, Catherine was making the most of the children's week with their father after Christmas to catch up on her writing. Her fiction seemed to be fading into banality compared with real life at the moment and she was struggling to get into her new novel.

She was sitting in her usual crouched position on her large office chair in her oversized writing cardigan, legs tucked under her. There was no way that she could have held down an office job, simply because sitting straight backed, feet on the floor, directly facing a computer was beyond her. There was something army-like about the position, disciplined, obedient, as if standing to attention, at the orders only of the commanding officer of the screen in front of you. It was probably more efficient, but her rebellious streak would have quickly sent her AWOL from the parade ground of the open space.

She'd definitely gone AWOL from her senses the previous week she thought, biting her lip as if to chastise herself for the smile that she could feel spreading over her face as she thought back to her ski fling. It had been cheesy, obvious, totally unromantic but she knew that she had used J-B more than he must think that he'd used her.

Once she'd overcome her initial shyness, or rather sheer embarrassment, she'd actually enjoyed it, enjoyed him. She'd felt young and alive as he'd glided expertly over the moguls of her body and had surprised herself as she'd performed freestyle moves that had her body and mind flipping and spinning. There was no doubt about it, shedding her clothes had shed years off her, had reminded her of the excitement life had to offer. Her husband had clearly never wanted to forego the fever, the trembling, the racing heart. Those symptoms that she had only endured during the flu, he had enjoyed without the side effects of a runny nose and a dull headache.

She had no idea what would happen next but decided that she would leave it all to life. Family planning clearly hadn't worked out for her.

She tried to concentrate on what she had just written but just then a skype call came in from her editor in London. Catherine felt like a schoolgirl being caught thinking about boys in class, about getting it on with the best looking boy in the year rather than getting on with her work.

Not that Vanessa, her editor, was the school ma'am type. Just the opposite, she'd probably gone around more times than the London Eye. But though she may be a staple on the capital's literary social scene with more verve and sparkle than the champagne glass that provided her arm candy most evenings, her reputation as one of the top editors in the country meant that she was revered by those under her, respected by those above her and regarded by the authors she nurtured as somewhere between a mythical goddess and a BFF.

As usual, she got to the point, the house style.

"Catherine darling, I'm not really convinced by that dating scene in chapter twelve."

Catherine had sent in a few pages before the holidays at Vanessa's request but hadn't been comfortable with what she'd written herself.

"I know. I couldn't get it right. Can you put a finger on it?"

While the accent was all London, the editor's look was a hundred percent Paris Left Bank. In her black top that her own mother would deign to use only to dust the house but that had probably set her editor back a few hundred quid in a French boutique in London's own little corner of France, and Yves Saint-Laurent tuxedo jacket, she could have stepped right out of *Les Editeurs* restaurant in Paris' sixth *arrondissement*. Her answer told Catherine that she had more than a bookish knowledge of the country.

"I don't know. I haven't been with any Frenchmen since a boy called Pierre stuck his tongue so far down my throat during a French exchange visit that he wasn't far off dipping it in the Paris sewers. God knows why they're so scatologically minded. Do you know that's actually a tourist attraction, the Paris sewers? Must be all that '*Merde*', '*Fait chier*' they keep on popping into their conversations." She shivered to herself at the thought "Urgh, the taste of *Gauloise* cigarettes and Hollywood chewing gum lingers still."

Catherine laughed as Vanessa pulled a face and straightened her jacket.

"But anyway, to get back to business, it comes over a bit too much like the American dating game. Could you inject a bit of *oh la la* into it?"

Catherine tried to wipe the thought of a less worldly-wise, sixteen-year old Vanessa in an emerald green Benetton jumper and a perm from her mind and turned back to her book.

"Are we talking about the scene where Susan isn't sure how far to go on the first date?"

"Yes, it's a bit first base, second base, just too American. Isn't there another rule book over there, another sport they use for inspiration for their love lives other than baseball?"

Skiing fleetingly came to Catherine's mind and she shifted in her seat to get rid of the rising warmth in her groin.

"I'll have to think about it. I'm only just back in the race myself."

She racked her brains for an idea.

"I suppose they take their lead from boules, someone throws in the little *cochonnet* ball, then all the players rub up as near to it as possible, touch it and own it, and evict their competitors."

Vanessa beamed.

"Now that sounds as if it has potential for getting up close and personal. Work on that."

"Ok I just need to ask around and find out how to get some of the action these days. I know some people are on dating sites, there are even some for married people. Imagine."

Her editor looked at her with something verging on pity in her eyes and Catherine suddenly felt very naïve.

"Just art imitating life darling."

At least there had been nothing virtual about her fling with J-B.

"It's not my idea of the art of seduction," she answered with a vehemence that made her blasé editor look up from the text message she was simultaneously typing noisily with the tips of her false nails.

"Look I don't care how you do it but sex up that scene a bit and come back to me with something, I'll give you three months max to finish the whole thing. Bye darling, off to a book launch, again. Lots of men for you darling. Maybe you need to come back over here. Buy British. Cheerio sweetie."

With that Catherine was left looking at her own face in the screen. Not a back cover shot look this morning, her skin vulnerably free of make-up and her long, unbrushed hair full of knots, she looked what she was, an almost forty something home alone with no one to make an effort for, not even the children.

But now she'd been given a mission, to find out how to find a man, even if it was only research for the sake of her book. According to Flo, who'd demanded a full report of her holiday fling and thirstily lapped up all the details, ski instructors apparently didn't count. It was too easy. That meant she would have to find another source to capture the authenticity of her character's love life. Real life apparently wasn't the reality any more. What had happened to her was just the exception that proved the rule. It was a fluke, a one-off, a remnant of another era of coupling. So Catherine switched screens and started googling for love, muttering "Twenty first century dating here I come. Let's lose my virtual virginity."

Quite a few site suggestions came up and she looked at them as if sizing up a line of men at a bar, not really knowing which to choose. She picked one that seemed to tout long-term relationships and not just short-term dalliances and started checking out the identity parade of merchandise that she could put into her basket. She eliminated the ones that looked too pornographic, sadomasochistic, fascistic, enigmatic, embryotic, egotistic, cirrhotic, celibatic, ballistic, arthritic, apathetic, alkalotic, unromantic, activistic, anaesthetic, antierotic, anaclitic, robotic, fanatic, sadistic, pathetic, narcissistic, hysteretic, syphilitic, voyeuristic, unrealistic, terroristic, sycophantic, racialistic, necromantic, mentalistic, manneristic and hypoplastic … and gradually realised that normalistic probably wasn't an option.

She found a backlit photo of herself that she hoped that no one would recognise and then got down to the job of filling in her profile.

She entered her real eye colour and fake hair colour, her actual height but made up her interests. But then she came to a halt. "What do you mean chest size?" she asked the nosey parker. Scrolling down the list she noticed that they didn't have "sagging" and was forced to lie. "Sexual preferences?" Well there's no beating around the bush there… she scrolled down further, I don't believe it, there actually is. "Who cares what I put anyway?" she mumbled to herself. "All in a day's work. It's not as if I'm going to actually meet any of them. I just want to extract their thoughts and motivations like some digital Mata Hari."

She clicked on *Enter* and felt instantly vulnerable. Of course she hadn't used her real name or given away any identifying information but she had a niggling feeling that while her life, or at least her love life, wasn't on the line, there was no getting away from the fact that it was now most decidedly online.

CHAPTER 36

Forget *boules*, this was bloody Wimbledon, thought Catherine as she checked her phone for messages for the umpteenth time that day. Two months into internet dating and she'd decided that the sport it best matched was tennis with its quick exchanges, each return ball to the opponent the other side of the screen either gently landing in their court to be assessed and played, smashing over the line to be lost somewhere in the crowd or lobbed into the air, with everyone hovering around to see where it would take them.

What had started as a kind of immersive work experience for her book soon had her doing overtime as soon as the children were tucked up and playing happy families in their sleep. That's when she would take her laptop to bed with her and respond to all the dating site messages. Not all, of course, some she would first bin all the 'ists' that belonged in the no-way category while taking note of the expressions they used, their approach and tone for use in her novel.

The problem was that her flirting history was still fossilised back in the age of the 'do you come here often'. She also remembered vaguely being a bit confused when a guy in the college bar asked her if her dad was a burglar because apparently he'd stolen the stars from the sky and put them in her eyes. Obviously that corny stuff had gone out with the ra-ra skirt but she needed the 2.0 version to put into her characters' mouth. It probably wouldn't do her love CV any harm to have them on file for future reference either.

So there she was now, in the middle of phase two, responding to some of the messages just to get a feel for the pace and level of the conversation. She was playing the role of lovelorn singleton with three of them, making up answers to reel them in, then keeping up the pretence and side-stepping any suggestions to meet up, speak on the phone or via skype.

It was easy for her, she just treated it as a dialogue in one of her novels, making up her part while someone else was writing the other half, picking up on their style, telling them what she thought they wanted to hear, being the person they wanted her to be, leading them up the garden path before slamming the front door in their faces.

Her true self only came out when talking to one of her new online friends, a guy who went as Frenchie. He hadn't put a proper photo of himself, an omission that immediately implied that he was no George Clooney, but he had intriguingly put a photo of his silhouette looking out at a mountain landscape. The overall effect gave the impression that he wanted someone to look together in the same direction with, someone to share the experience, or the ride. She liked that. Or else he really was swipe-left ugly of course.

As soon as she logged in, she received a message from Frenchie. Was he lying in wait for a sign of her presence? She took a sip of the herbal tea she'd been on since January after the festive excesses, Romain's autumn wining and dining and the long, wet, tear and vodka sodden summer of depression and started reading.

***

A few days after submitting a new draft Vanessa was skyping her again. This time the editor's dark-rimmed glasses and Chanel-red lips were filling the screen, and she leaned forward further as if she would kiss Catherine if she could.

"Love the new scene darling. It's got more of the French connection. Don't know where you got your inspiration, but it works."

"Actually I found this online dating site," Catherine filled her in.

"No! You actually did it darling! Shouldn't you have a sweet sixteen party to celebrate your new-found maturity?"

"To be honest, to get that chapter I had a few dodgy close encounters of the online kind."

"Oh give me the dirt, darling. I love these kinds of stories…"

"Well one was with a guy who called himself snailman and who was really keen for me to be Russian for some reason and kept on asking how long my legs were. He kept on calling me Catherine the Great."

Vanessa gave her husky laugh.

"And you didn't meet him? Next time slug your snailman in my direction. He can't be slimier than a lot of the guys I've met in my time!"

"No but I did hit it off with someone else." Catherine hesitated, before admitting "I'm actually meeting him tonight for the first time in the flesh. In an hour's time actually."

Vanessa could hardly contain her excitement.

"Oh my God what's he like?"

"To be honest I haven't even seen a proper photo."

"Well, he can't be worse than that guy you were married to. I never told you my lovely but he was never good enough for you. At all those literary gatherings, he'd always be out the back smoking with the waiters rather than standing proudly on your arm. I should have said it sooner maybe. But you're well rid of him. Just ask this one if he's heard of Rushdie, Frantzen or that French Houllebecq guy before you go too far. If I were you, I'd even give him a literary quiz before you meet up tonight. Anyway, brave move going photoless."

Catherine didn't really want to explain about the back shot and the "shared vision" angle she'd convinced herself of and played down her hopes.

"Hey it's just for fun. I didn't really ever mean to meet up but … I don't know, it was strange with this one, I just felt I'd known him forever."

Her editor was curious.

"So how are you going to know who he is? Newspaper under the arm, flower in the lapel job?"

"No he said he'd be wearing a blue jumper, and ..."

But Catherine was interrupted by the sound of the doorbell …

"Oh that's the babysitter. Have to dash. You never know, this could be the first day of the rest of my life."

"*Ciao* darling," answered Vanessa. "Just tell me what happens next… I'll hold off printing until you've got the ending you want."

CHAPTER 37

Tom, the faithful barista-cum-babysitter couldn't have been more flummoxed if he'd been writing the name Marilyn on a paper cup only to look up and see the starlet standing there in the flesh ordering a latte. Catherine, the mature woman of his dreams had opened the door to him and was a vision in hotpants. She may have had tights on underneath and boots up to her knees but the sight of his object of desire in such unusually sexy attire brought on a moment of …

"Mrs Dupont!" he exclaimed, then pulled himself together, "Hi, I'm here, hope I'm not late. How are the kids?"

He was hoping for a chat with her before she left but she was already reaching for a long khaki-coloured suede coat and he felt a pang of relief at the thought that she wouldn't be sharing that sight with everyone on the way to wherever she was going, but the respite was short-lived…

"Hey Tom. Have to dash. Hot date!"

He was crushed.

She rushed to the TV room to give the children a cuddle and curfew instructions before hurtling out of the door, grabbing her bag on the way, and shouting her thanks behind her.

Tom shut the door and leant back against it, already missing the days when Catherine would come into the coffee shop with that hounded look on her face and cower behind her large Americano, as if sheltering from unwanted observation and comments, looking as if she was hiding from something or someone or had something to be ashamed of.

A timid smile from her when he crossed her gaze had been enough to reveal a kind nature that someone had psychologically steamrollered into a petrified impassivity. He had hoped to dare that he could in some way or another entice back the gentle features of her face and redefine those delicate contours. Unfortunately for him, it clearly wasn't going to be his place to lure out those dimples, not tonight at least.

* * *

The truth was that Catherine's dramatic exit had nothing to do with excitement. She had fled the house in a state of panic, knowing that if she started to think about what she was doing, she would be out of her ridiculous hotpants and back in her comfiest flannel reindeer pyjamas within minutes.

Despite seemingly boasting about her chivalrous meeting, as the French put it, she was starting to think that this emoticon-based relationship should have remained the adult Tamagotchi game that it was, one that she could have fed and nurtured virtually, switching it off at any time by yanking the game card from the slot.

She had downed a glass of red to give her some Dutch courage but now, as the taxi climbed up the by now familiar bends to Max's restaurant, her nerves and her curiosity were going head to head in an epic battle to the finish.

The umpire in her head told her that she had chosen Max's restaurant for that very purpose, to give her the safety of a familiar presence to save her skin if Frenchie turned out to be two drumsticks short of a *coq au vin*.

But the nerves were gaining ground and her curiosity was about to be taken down for the count when she realised that the taxi had stopped at the restaurant entrance. Her nerves were foiled by the driver opening the door, and her writer's discipline forced her back onto her feet and tipped her out onto the red carpet leading up to the restaurant.

The front door was already being held open by Paul, the doorman, who greeted her by her name when he saw her emerge from the car. Now she had no choice. Any change of heart she might have envisaged had been floored by a brutal knock-out. But that had only been the warm-up. She was about to step into the ring for the real face-to-face encounter.

Shedding her outer suede skin and handing it to the awaiting suit-clad *chef de salle*, she felt the red wine take over and got into character as she strode out into the atmosphere of the footlights created by the line of candle-lit tables.

She spotted the man in the blue jumper straight away. Her co-star was sitting by the floor-to-ceiling window, busy examining the bottle of wine that he had pulled from the ice bucket for a closer look. He looked anywhere between 45 and 50, maybe older than she had expected, but had a distinguished air about him. He didn't have that outdoor ruggedness the mountain-framed photo had suggested, was more sophisticated than she had imagined, but going by his intense scrutiny of the bottle, who knows, in the photo he may have been looking out over a vineyard scaling the steep valleys of Savoie.

But she had to make her move before Max saw her and caused her to deviate from her target. She made a b-line for the table.

At that point, Max came out of the kitchen to dutifully give his guests a sighting of the star chef and was about to approach her with open arms when he saw her slide into the seat opposite the blue-jumpered diner and unleash her pre-prepared French spiel.

"J'espère que je ne vous ai pas trop fait attendre," Catherine seemed to be purring, trying to charm her way out of her lateness.

This wasn't the same Catherine who enjoyed laid-back dinners with Romain in demure little black dresses, Max thought, as he saw her flirtatiously throwing back her hair. But there was no stopping her. He was growing increasingly bemused as he witnessed the scene. Damn it. Were he not the renowned chef that he was, he would have been tempted to take out his phone and record it all to show Romain later.

The man seemed rather taken aback by the arrival of this guest. And Catherine was clearly surprised by his surprise. Not sure how to respond, the man Catherine thought of as Frenchie, given that they had not yet had time to shed their pseudos, simply spluttered an American-accented *"Mademoiselle ..."*

Catherine immediately took this to be a sign that her French period, which had admittedly ended rather badly, could finally be put behind her and that pastures new were awaiting her.

"Oh, you're American! But your French was perfect on chat. Or are you Canadian? Bilingual? So you were being ironic when you used Frenchie! So brains, beauty and humour."

Rather short for breath after her hysterical monologue, Catherine laughed in a way that she hoped to be sexy yet intelligent in a Katherine Hepburn kind of way and looking for a way to move on the conversation grabbed a menu.

"Have you already chosen?" she asked.

Making the most of the woman's studied examination of his album-like menu, the lone diner used his eyes to Morse code his desperation to Max on the other side of the dining room, who, getting the message, started making his way over.

When she looked up, Catherine saw the chef standing at their table and with some relief, given the distinct and rather disappointing lack of reaction of any kind from her date, gave both a dazzling smile before taking up the reins of the conversation again.

"Ah voila Max," she said her eyes darting rather manically between both men. "May I present you to Max, the best chef in the city ... and beyond. Max, this is ... oh God I've just realised that I only know you as Frenchie," she giggled like a Japanese schoolgirl caught with her knee-high socks down, "Max, this is Frenchie."

At that point, things started to move in slow motion for Catherine as she saw Jumperman shrug his shoulders at Max and Max wordlessly answer him by half closing his eyes and gesture with his hand in a way that said "Don't worry, I'll deal with this psychopath." He then bent over and discretely whispered in Catherine's ear.

"Catherine, I think you've made a mistake, this guy is from Parker's Wine Guide. I don't know who you're meeting, but it could be the other man in the blue jumper, sitting behind you, shaking uncontrollably with laughter with tears pouring down his face."

She let what Max had just told her sink in. Then, mustering as much dignity as she could, she got up and looked straight into the Parker's representative now sparkling eyes and, with a performance that would have earned her at least a 98 out of a 100 had she been a bottle of Oddbins' finest, said,

"Mr Parker, or whatever your name is, may I just say how much I love your guide and its contents, especially in their concrete configuration, and that that particular hue of blue is a perfect pairing for your full-bodied and very palatable form and I'm sure that, had you been the man I was supposed to be meeting, and had it gone any further, that your bouquet would have been strikingly bold and musky and that you would have had a very pleasant, lingering finish. I wish you a pleasant evening."

With that, she turned on her heels and immediately came to an abrupt halt. The other blue-jumpered man in the room, sitting at the next table, and who had somehow escaped her notice when she had first walked in, had the dating desirability of a Smurf. But at least she could cut the femme fatale act. The mystery was over. The familiarity now made sense. She parked herself on the chair, tugging down her hotpants.

"Of all the Frenchies in all the towns in all of France, you had to talk to me on-line."

Jacques was still trying not to choke on his own hilarity but managed to come out with his usual insult-tinged charming response.

"I think I just fell in love with you all over again watching you doing that over there. Why did I ever think I was bored?"

She crossed her arms and legs and arched an eyebrow.

"Oh, and are those hot pants new?" he added.

She glared back at him. "Don't you dare think that this is the beginning of a beautiful friendship."

But Jacques had obviously been thinking things through since seeing that his internet date was his own wife, estranged though she may be.

"Come on *bébé*, we were together for years, the computer put us back together again. You can't argue with science."

But Catherine was having none of it and hissed back.

"Don't they have virus protection on those things? Creep firewalls? Ex-husband filters? God I need a drink."

She caught Max's commiserating eye and he left his pans to bring her back a glass of much needed wine, the open bottle in his other hand.

"With the compliments of Parker," and with a nasty look at Jacques, "My choice."

With that he poured her a glass of Bâtard-Montrâchet Grand Cru and ignoring Jacques' extended glass, turned on his heels and went back to work.

"I'll drink to that," said Catherine, twisting round to raise her glass in apology to Mr Parker's man behind her before turning back to face her past.

"Look Jacques, I'm not having dinner with you. It's over. What you've done in the past months since our separation has been almost worse than your infidelity. It's just one example after another of how you want to control me, suffocate me, shame me and hurt me."

But Jacques was clearly out on the town to *"conclure"* that evening, even though he'd clearly forgotten that he'd already 'got lucky' 15 years earlier when he first set his eyes on Catherine. The deal had been signed and sealed, until he'd violated the terms of the agreement.

"Just give me one more chance. There must be something left …"

The drama of the evening was starting to get to Catherine and with what she hoped would be a finale she gave him her coldest look.

"You killed that something," she said, "I waited for the resurrection but it isn't coming. I obviously don't have Jesus in my heart. Judas hit too hard this time."

"So it's over?"

Catherine kept her voice low but determined.

"It could be the worse decision that I've taken in my life. For me, for my children and for you. I don't know. But I can't imagine putting myself back in the hands of my torturer. It would smack of Stockholm syndrome. You made me suffer for too long and above all exploited all my weaknesses. You never really supported my writing, you probably haven't even read most of it. You just liked the idea of me holed up with the children but financially solvent while you had the freedom to screw your way around Europe. You kept me in my place, making me feel fat, ugly and unworthy, while you swaggered and strutted around as if the white stuff you were selling was cocaine rather than bog roll. You took your mistress on weekends away while I minded the children. And you've taken my dream of a family away, while you had your dirty-minded flings. You've just destroyed it all. Destroyed me."

But Jacques still seemed to think that destiny had brought them back together. "We can rebuild our dreams together. One last try."

Catherine was having none of it.

"The 'WE' hasn't existed for a long time. To be honest I sometimes think that we were the victims of an experiment among university students to foster European unification. I mean did you know anyone who actually did any work on their Erasmus year out? We were probably all just on a mass date. Which means that ours was an arranged marriage while under the influence of the beer-fuelled propaganda. Just a common market, but in the end maybe that exchange programme was the only thing we had in common. Maybe the Euro-sceptics are right, maybe I will be better off on my own, out of the 'Union'."

"We were the union of 2 beings who loved each other passionately. Too much is at stake. I don't want to live with any regrets."

"Nor do I, that's why I can't wake up to see your face every morning. You can skype her now to tell her you're a free man if she still wants you. You lived your life all this time. Now I need to live mine."

"But I love you. I admire you. I just couldn't tell you. You were just too perfect … Your discipline, your enthusiasm, your beauty, your kindness, your patience, your sociability, your professionalism, your desires, your passions, your class, your maternal side with our children … your large breasts."

Jacques leered at her, forgetting all the high-minded declarations leading up to that moment.

Catherine looked at him with a pitying look. It wasn't working. The lights had been switched off and the door closed.

"Don't spoil it…"

That was when the music suddenly seemed to come out in sympathy with her ex-husband and a familiar song came on. He looked at her with imploring eyes.

"Will you give me this dance then … and afterwards, if you want, I'll leave you alone?"

She hesitated, how many times had this stop-and-start dialogue been going on? But then again, she thought, even on death row prisoners have a last meal request. She led him to a secluded corner of the restaurant feeling as if she was taking a lamb to the slaughter, though fully aware that the wolf was probably lying in wait inside.

She then let him guide her around the makeshift dancefloor to the doleful laments of Jacques Brel's *'Ne me quitte pas'*.

Catherine, by now weak on her liquid diet, could do nothing more than hold onto Jacques and grant him the last dance. Then, she whispered in his ear.

"Will you take me home?"

CHAPTER 38

With what she hoped to be yet another apologetic glance at the innocent victim of her internet dating fiasco and an 'I'll explain later' look at Max who had been keeping tabs on her from his open kitchen overlooking the restaurant, Catherine let Paul help her on with her coat and walked out.

The cold air felt like a well-deserved slap on her face for putting herself in such a ridiculous situation.

"I'm parked over here," Jacques said as he walked past her towards the car park.

By the time she got there, he was there holding the passenger door open for her. Her senses went into alert. He'd never done that before. Just like the dancing. Hadn't she been clear? There was no going back. So why was he being such a gentleman? Something he'd picked up from having a mistress probably, she sneered to herself, and got into the car without thanking him.

Neither of them said anything as the car, Jacques' company French saloon, financed by spools of spent toilet paper, left behind the fairytale lights of the restaurant on the hill and headed back down through the dark alleyways of the old town.

The area was unhospitable at this late hour, even threatening when some lone figure would emerge from the sinister *traboules* that turned this part of the city into a gruyere cheese of secret passageways.

The silence that reigned between them seemed to imply that the jury was out. The arguments had been aired, the counterarguments expounded, the evidence exposed. A tense courtroom atmosphere held them in suspense inside the car, as if a final judgement would be delivered as soon as this journey came to an end.

Maybe that's why Jacques seemed to be in no hurry. While his erratic and video-game style driving had often been a source of marital tiffs, he was now driving through the city and back towards their suburb at a hearse's pace. He slowed down as he approached each light, as if willing them to turn red. He stopped respectfully at each give way sign, even when he had priority coming from the left, almost hoping that a car would force them to stall their journey. He seemed to be drawing out the death throes of their marriage.

Catherine could feel him throwing glances at her from time to time but she looked straight ahead, like the body in the coffin at her own wake.

After an excruciatingly long time, Jacques could delay their arrival no longer and they finally drew up at the house. The tomblike silence of their last commute was broken by Jacques, who had clearly seen it as a sign of a possible resurrection.

"So can I come in for coffee?"

Catherine turned to face him for the first time since stepping into the car keeping one door on the handle.

"I've switched to tea," she said.

"I don't know if tea is more compatible with computers," Jacques tried to humour his way into the marital home.

But she was having none of it.

"Skype me then, and we'll find out. *Bonne nuit* Jacques."

Jacques' frustration got the better of him.

"So you're going through with it? One not very youthful indiscretion and you give up on almost twenty years of *entente cordiale*?"

"It's what I've seen of you since the separation that's diluted the 'cordial'."

The turn the conversation was taking was making the air inside the confined space of the car toxic.

"Then the game is over Catherine."

Catherine gasped for air at the deadly tone and answered with the same virulence.

"If you hadn't started playing around in the first place, we wouldn't be here."

But he wasn't listening to her, intent on turning himself into the poor victim who had no choice but to defend himself.

"The gloves are off."

Catherine was struck again by the vicious and vindictive side of his character that he had kept so well hidden for all the years she's known him but she didn't want to show that she was impressed by all his swashbuckling.

"Oh please, don't come over all Scarlet Pimpernel on me. What are you going to do? Throw down the gauntlet and challenge me to a duel?"

Not waiting for an answer she tried to get out of the car but he grabbed her and put his face so close to hers that she thought that he was trying to kiss her into submission. But only scorn came out of his mouth.

"Forget your damned Waterloo. This is one battle the French are going to win. And French rules apply."

Catherine pushed him off her and struggled with her belt as she tried to make it out of the car.

"I'll tell the kids it's definitive tomorrow."

But Jacques was continuing with his man scorned act.

"I expect everyone else knows already. Your friends and the twittering classes."

The separation had hardly been a bed of roses before but Catherine felt that this was a turning point and that things were only just starting to get ugly.

"Well I'm definitely unliking you more with every passing second," was the only thing she could think to say as a pang of fear took grip of her and she slammed the car door shut.

Even though she pulled the gate shut behind her she couldn't help but throw glances over her shoulder until she got to the front door in case he'd followed her. It wasn't until she heard the car start up and rouse the street with its tyre-screeching exit that she could finally relax and be thankful that this battle at least was over.

She was glad that Tom was waiting for her inside. His smiling face looking up at her from the sofa as she walked in calmed her down.

"Hi Tom, how did it go?"

A mischievous twinkle lit up his eyes.

"Shouldn't I be the one asking you that? Everything was fine here. No problems. They're great kids you know."

"Yes I know. I'm lucky to have them. Are you working tomorrow?"

His hopes already high after seeing her return so early from her date and, more importantly, alone, he thought he'd grab his chance.

"Yes, barista by day, babysitter by night. Do you want me to moonlight for you as well?"

Catherine was probably thinking that he was joking as she didn't seem at all taken aback by his suggestion.

"Thanks, but I need to come back down to earth. And no, I don't need it to move for me. I've had enough action for a while."

She opened the door with a tired smile.

"Night Tom."

"Night Mrs Dupont," he said and slunk off into the night.

The door closed again on another man's dreams. That's all she seemed to be able to do at the moment, close doors on everyone, shut everyone out from her life.

For a split second she was tempted to go after him. She wasn't that dim. She knew exactly what Tom had been suggesting. He would have stayed to cheer her up in a shot. But that was it. It would only have been a shot, a shot in the dark and while having a strong pair of arms around her sounded tempting, he deserved more than a mature woman using him as a comfort blanket.

Instead, she went to check on the children. She couldn't help but smile when she saw Manon sprawled across the bed still in her princess dress in a position of unconditional surrender to the sandman, the sheet swathed like a toga around her. The remains of the play lipstick turned her mouth into a partially rubbed out drawing and the overall impression was of a Disney princess after the wrap party.

She took off the plastic sparkly shoes with their little heel, gave her a gentle kiss and left her to her dreams of happy ever after, knowing that they were going to be shattered the next day. "I'm sorry," she whispered with the tears streaming down her eyes. "I'm so, so sorry."

Arthur was curled up at the bottom of the bed, his duvet keeping only the floor warm. Catherine carefully draped it over him and put him back in a more comfortable position. He groaned but didn't wake up.

They were so perfect. They deserved more than what lay in store for them. But they also deserved more realistic role models than anything they had in their video collection. They needed a mother who stood up for her right to be respected. And they needed a father who took responsibility for his actions. The French had a great way of putting it, you just didn't 'spit in the soup'. You didn't bite the hand that was there to caress you.

In the master bedroom, the one whose master had found a mistress, she thought back to that night in July, seven months earlier, when she'd discovered the betrayal. The entire vocabulary still made her sick. Saying that he had 'cheated on her' made it sound as if he'd been playing a rigged card game on her naked body, and 'fooling around' gave the impression that he'd had too much fun behind her back, just adding insult to injury. And injury it was, a big gaping wound that was taking a long time to heal.

But the honeymoon period of their separation was over. If Jacques had thought that it had been a seven-month itch, that the scratching and clawing were over, then at least now he knew that it hadn't just been a matter of Catherine getting his infidelity out of her system.

The next step was to switch off the life support machine of their marriage for good. She would relaunch the divorce proceedings the next day and really get on with her life.

With that she crawled under the bedclothes and cried her heart out in a draining detox.

CHAPTER 39

The mist that packed the valley of the River Saone like cotton wool was starting to lose steam, freeing the days from their daily dose of greyness, gradually liberating the city's population from those beastly layers of wool, faux fur and, for the lucky ones, goose feather.

The regenerated river banks with their boardwalks, cycle paths and playgrounds were timidly emerging from their winter hibernation and again drawing the shorn, skinned and plucked urbanites out of their winter lethargy.

Catherine definitely had a spring in her step as she walked along the fast-flowing waters to her appointment with her lawyer. She'd decided that the sooner they were divorced, the better it would be for everyone.

She felt confident in the future, and looked it, having put on a formal business suit for her encounter, one that she hadn't put on for years because of the extra baby weight. When it had slipped effortlessly over her hips and buttoned up without straining at the seams she'd thanked God for the divorce diet, the easiest of them all, the one that just made you too sick to your stomach to eat.

Or maybe God had nothing to do with it, she thought. It could well be a clever ploy by nature to make you desirable for the next partner. But whatever, whether divine intervention or animal instinct, she felt ready to face the world.

She was called into the lawyer's office almost as soon as she arrived. After going through the formalities of stipulating her divorce wishlist that would be submitted to the judge, her counsel, a bespectacled forty-something in an expensive suit and those awful white collared shirts favoured by American stockbrokers, closed the file, put his pen down and looked at her intently.

"Just one last thing."

Catherine stopped putting her notes away in her leather and sequin Vanessa Bruno bag and looked up.

"Yes, what?"

"You can't make any false move," the lawyer continued.

Catherine wasn't sure she understood. What did he mean by false move?

Seeing her confusion, he continued.

"What I mean is that he still has a possibility of turning the proceedings into a divorce for fault."

Catherine's confusion only grew.

"But how? I'm divorcing because of his adultery."

"Yes, but you've opted for mutual consent, not fault, for the time being, which means that you also have to, how can I put it, behave, or at least make sure that no one knows that you're misbehaving."

Catherine couldn't believe the hypocrisy of what she was hearing.

"But I'm separated and have been for months. I can't put my life on hold. A divorce can take years."

"I'm afraid that you're still married in the eyes of the law Madame Dupont."

Catherine could hardly speak. What kind of country was this, where adultery was not only condoned but almost expected, but where once you called it by its name you were the one being caught with your clothes off and held up in scorn and ridicule!

"As your lawyer I have to warn you that's all. I hope that you haven't done anything that could put you in a delicate position already," he continued, leaning forward slightly as if avid for a lurid confession so that he could absolve her of her sins. It would explain the white collar at least.

Catherine turned a slightly darker shade of pink as she thought back to her short-lived skiing holiday romance. But the lawyer must have picked up on the icy glint in her eye and brought the meeting to an end with a terse warning.

"Just be careful."

***

Too angry to drive home immediately, Catherine decided that she needed a sounding board and headed for Tom's coffee house. She crossed the red iron footbridge, the skip in her step now transformed into a determined stride, making the structure tremble with every step. She felt a childish urge to jump up and down on it so hard as to make it collapse into the fast-flowing murky water below, taking her with it and putting an end to this farce.

Tom saw her come in and immediately felt a double espresso moment coming on. He had it ready for her before she reached the counter. With a silent nod of gratitude, Catherine downed it and went to sit at one of the tables in the back.

Tom was serving the customers, being his usual charming self, handing over each cup or paper goblet with a smile and a kind word. As soon as he found a window he popped over to his favourite customer with a soothing cappuccino to bring her down from her high and put it in front of her without a word, not sure what had put her in this dour-faced frame of mind.

Glancing back to check that there were no customers waiting, he sat down in the seat next to her and leaned under the hair that was cascading down onto the table and hiding the face he'd come to like so much.

"What's up?"

"I don't like people telling me what I can and can't do," she answered quizzically.

"Oh my God. Is it because of the espresso? I'm sorry if I took it for granted that that's what you wanted."

Tom was devastated at the thought that he was in his friend's bad books.

But his answer brought a smile to Catherine's face.

"No it's not that you dipstick! You're the best thing that's happened to me all day. No, it's just the lawyer."

Catherine was on a roll and Tom could only sit there and listen to her gripe with the French injustice system.

"You see, apparently now that I'm a single woman but not yet divorced I'm in this kind of chastity-belt purgatory where I'm supposed to play the Virgin Mary until the principle of the divorce is accepted by the judge! Can you imagine, in this day and age, in the twenty first century I have some lawyer I've only just met and who knows me only through my divorce papers telling me what to do. It's like being a teenager again, under some kind of tutelage. And then I have some all-powerful judge I've never seen in my life telling me how to live my life! Who does this invisible judge think he is, the Wizard of Oz? But if I as much as flash my ruby slippers at a lion, tin man or a bloody scarecrow I'm the one who gets dubbed the wicked witch. My God, just you sitting there next me could be taken as proof that I'm the harlot in this farce."

Tom immediately stood up and stepped back, not wanting to make her life even more difficult. But that only made Catherine look up and smile. She extended her hand and drew him back to the table.

"You obviously don't know me. No one tells me what I can and can't do. Not even the French legal system."

She looked him straight in the eye.

"So what are you doing on Friday night? The children have been invited for a sleepover at a friend's house."

CHAPTER 40

As early spring burst forth into summer, Catherine put up two fingers at the Gallic hypocrisy, flew in the face of caution and cast her clout before her divorce was out.

After all, what had being 'good' brought her? What had been her prize for being a committed homemaker, a dedicated mother and loyal wife, for bowing to convention? He'd been out there thinking "stuff the wife" while she'd been home alone stuffing mushrooms.

Her rebellious streak, the one her parents knew so well, her abhorrence of tradition that had prompted her mother to express her surprise as she saw her settle down as a married woman, had been dared out of its retirement.

Tom was in seventh heaven. Not only would Catherine now spend hours working on her book in the café but now a coffee wasn't the only thing she took away with her. Catherine wasn't completely crazy and knew that she was playing a dangerous game and so they tried to be discreet, were careful not to be seen in public, and would meet up in Tom's modest apartment at unlikely hours, steering away from Catherine's suburban fishbowl.

But the cloak and dagger stuff only added to the excitement. They were in a world of their own, far removed from reality, with no future and no past, only the present, and the feeling that they were carousing for a cause, or rather against the perverted morality of the system.

By early summer Catherine was still waiting for the judge to set a date for the divorce hearing. The frustration was setting in, especially as the early summer heatwave was making Tom's non-air-conditioned apartment too hot for comfort. She'd had enough of the noises that would rise up from the street below and crash in through the open windows to disturb their blissful sleep. He seemed to live in a closed circuit of clamour in his part of the city, the commotion of the market stalls being put up in the morning giving way only to the shouts and back-up alarms of the binmen and their lorries, before making place for the pandemonium of the traffic during the day, which passed on the baton to the aperitif crowd at sundown, some of whom turned into the clubbers finding their way home by echolocation in the early hours and who drunkenly exchanged greetings with the first market traders warming their vocal chords in readiness for another day of banter.

Catherine was also starting to crave her own crisp fitted sheets rather than Tom's crinkled covers ironed only by the movement of their bodies as they metaphorically made love over the perverted laws of the *Republique*.

So one morning, after waking up from an unrestful sleep to find that the mosquitoes had been playing apprentice acupuncturist with her body, she invited him over to her house. The children were staying with friends for the night and she had the place to herself.

Looking forward to being able to spend an evening with her lover in the comfortable surroundings of her own home, she took a long bath, put on a pretty summer dress, lit candles around the house and started making a romantic dinner for both of them.

She felt light and carefree in her cool stone-walled kitchen. Jacques had been keeping away. She only saw him fleetingly when he picked up or dropped off the children on his weekend with them. Her book was written and in the process of being printed, and Tom had given her hope that she had a future, that maybe she wouldn't end up a bitter old hag in a bottle-strewn flat after all. She didn't exactly consider him as the love of her life, but at least he had restored her love for life.

The doorbell interrupted her thoughts and Catherine rushed to answer it. She pulled him in, acting out of passion but also because of the Damocles sword that could fall and cut her thin thread of happiness at any time. Her neighbours had eyes, ears and tongues that sometimes wagged as hard as the tails of their blasted Chihuahuas.

Before he could say anything, Catherine pinned Tom against the key rack, but he didn't care if the key to the garden shed was digging into the nape of his neck as he relished every moment of this domestic bliss. He was only too happy to be the guest for once as she frisked him for the gift she had coming to her.

They were still kissing passionately in the hallway, Catherine leaning back half way across the large square hall table holding a vase of flowers and a pocket emptier as Tom poured his passion into her, when the doorbell rang. They ignored it, willing whoever it was to go away. Someone pressed on the bell again, and again, becoming more insistent as the heat was turned up on the table. When they heard the knocking on the door, the fire was finally put out and they looked at each other.

That's when they heard Jacques' voice on the other side of the door.

"I know you're in there. And I know you're not alone. Do I have to remind you that you're still a married woman? You're committing adultery. In my bed."

Tom found that to be hilarious and pointed to the table.

"Well he's got that wrong at least."

Then in a kind of a multimedia attack, the bell rang, the door knocker was activated and Catherine's telephone whirred into life at the same time. She couldn't move, petrified by the thought that her still husband and lover were only metres apart, separated by less than 10 centimetres of oak.

"Shit. It's Jacques. Oh my God, what have I got myself into," she started asking herself. "When did I turn into a femme fatale? I'm supposed to be an author, not a character in some kind of kinky French art house film."

Jacques' muffled voice seemed to answer her.

"If you don't open this door I'll find another way in. *Putain*. You're my wife. That's my wife in there. You're mine. You belong to me."

Tom was still finding it funny at that point, especially with the grotesque comment he'd just heard.

"So this is the guy who cheated on you yeah?"

But when Jacques started tapping on the window, both of them ducked behind the reassuringly solid hall table.

"Right, I'm phoning the police," said Catherine and embarked on some kind of boot-camp crawl across the cold flagstones to fetch her telephone from her handbag without being seen from any window.

As Catherine dialled a number and started talking volubly and gesticulating wildly towards the front door, Tom sighed, banged his head in frustration against the table leg and started to button up his shirt. Then he got up, blew out the candles all around him and, at his married mistress' behest, went to hide in her son's bedroom.

Five minutes later, the knocking on the door was accompanied by an announcement that the gendarmes were there. Catherine opened the door tentatively with the latch still on in case her ex had acquired impersonating skills in the past year or so. He'd certainly showed promise as a husband impersonator.

She came face to face with her old friend, St Desirée's *chef de la gendarmerie* with the Brummie accent, who was clearly not yet suffering from amnesia.

"Aha, it is you *madame*. I thought I recognised this address. What is the problem this time?"

Dismay was sprawled all over Catherine's face.

"Oh, I thought I'd called for support."

"If you are having marital problems *madame*, maybe you should be calling your Marriage Guidance Counsellor, not us. We are not English. We are not the Household Cavalry."

Catherine thought that she owed him an explanation at least.

"I called you because my soon-to-be ex-husband was banging on my door and threatening to break in. He wouldn't go away and he said that he would break a window."

But the old boys' club was out in force again tonight.

"Why did you not just open the door? France is a civilised country *madame*. This is not an American film. You don't have to have doors blown down, windows shattered, explosions resound. Here we are adults, we talk, we discuss over a glass of wine, reach an understanding, live and let live."

Just then a sneeze could be heard from upstairs and the gendarme narrowed his eyes as he leaned forward to peer for the truth in Catherine's face.

"Aha but maybe you had a reason not to let him in. … If *madame* is not alone, why does she need us? Does she not have a superhero to deal with her evil husband?"

God he was antagonistic this little bloated civil servant, so Catherine decided to go for it.

"Look I'm on my own and I'm telling you it was scary. He wouldn't go away. I thought he would hurt me. He was very angry. Maybe he's still out there. Can't you take a look? I don't feel safe. And I don't think that the British Embassy will be too happy if something happens to one of their citizens and you failed to protect them!"

She decided to bluff her way to a result.

"The British consul is a personal friend. Do I need to phone him to tell him that the French gendarmerie isn't taking my call seriously?"

With an exasperated look on his face, he turned to his two subordinates and ordered them to take a look around the garden and check all the windows. Off they went with their torches, their lack of haste and motivation clearly showing that they thought it all a waste of their time and effort.

But after only a few minutes, angry voices were heard outside and the *chef de gendarmerie* raised a rather intrigued eyebrow. As they turned towards the open front door they saw Jacques being marched off the grounds by an officer, followed by his father with a GoPro on his head and a wide lensed camera around his neck, tugged along by another official.

Catherine had a Eureka moment. For weeks now she'd had the impression that she was being followed but had shrugged it off as a figment of her imagination. But then the flashbacks invaded her. It had been her former father-in-law with the mismatched beard in that bar, with the dark glasses in that supermarket queue, dressed as a caretaker at school, even camouflaged in a burka in the beautician's waiting room … and then it struck her, yes even on that ski slope. Not many people of his age wore a helmet when skiing, let alone one with a GoPro perched on top of it. My God she'd been so naïve.

She was brought out of her musings and head banging against the door when she realised that Tom had his arms around her …groping for the latch as he tried to open it.

"What are you doing?" she asked. "You're not going are you?"

"Look Mrs D.," she's clearly lost her status as Catherine. "I just don't want to be involved."

The idea of being alone in the house sent her into a panic and she pleaded with him to stay, after all she needed his protection.

"But Jacques may come back," she argued.

"Exactly. That's why I have to go."

Catherine tried the macho card.

"What do you mean? Are you saying that you're scared of him?"

But Tom was a metrosexual of another generation and Harrison Ford wasn't his role model.

"I'm just a peace-loving philosophising barista Mrs D. I like you a lot, really a lot, but I can't get into fights with irate husbands. I can't be cited as another man in a divorce. This is just too mind-blowing for me."

"For me too," said Catherine bitterly. "I write drama and don't really want to live it. But I see that gentlemen only exist in novels."

Tom put on his baseball hat and sunglasses and hid his face with his voluminous chequered Keffiyeh.

"Great superhero disguise yellowman."

Tom looked sheepish and left with a "Sorry Mrs D."

Catherine could do nothing but look at him steal down the garden path towards the gate with his head down. He peeked around the hedge in both directions before legging it down the road. Without looking back. She closed the door quickly, realising that she was alone. Again.

***

Up the road in the village Jacques and his father were sneaking out of the gendarmerie in much the same demeanour as Tom, collars up, heads down, just in case anyone saw them. They'd only been given a warning, the gendarmes being sympathetic to Jacques' cause. But still, it was a bit embarrassing being caught stalking your wife, Jacques thought to himself. He felt like that Peter Sellers detective guy in those films his wife loved so much, but which he'd never really got his head around. Damned British humour.

The night had been a bit of a failure. He'd come away with no evidence of anyone being in the house with Catherine but he had a gut feeling that he would have found the proof he needed if only she hadn't phoned the damned police.

His father dropped him off at his bleak bachelor pad before heading back up to the Beaujolais.

He was too wound up to sleep so opened a beer and his computer. He tried to skype his ex-mistress. There was no answer. He logged onto his dad's dating website but was in no mood for small talk. Especially with all the pop-up banners offering him attractive women online and enough excitement to keep him up all night.

But he felt himself drowning in the cesspit of sleaze, that of his own making, the moral mud wrestling with his own wife and the sheer banality of the laptop lap dancing kind.

He banged down the cover. He was so tired that even attempting the barely one metre that separated the bed from his tip of a desk, littered with dirty plates and empty scrunched up cans dripping cigarette ash-infused brown water, seemed too much of an effort. For how long again would he have to live like this? He'd had a home, a family, a wife. He decided there and then, if he couldn't have her, or the kids, then there was one thing he would recover.

What did the bitch used to say, "an Englishman's home is his castle"? Well the next battle was to take the *putain de* castle.

***

Behind the solid walls of her fortress, Catherine wanted something more. She wanted home sweet home. Not a home, but to go home. Back to where having a problem meant being forced to choose between strawberry and raspberry jam on her scone, between reading the instructions in Welsh or English at the cash point, between daring to go out without an umbrella or playing it safe with a kagool.

After coming back down to land with a bang after her solo flight of fancy, she wanted to escape the scorched earth she had left in her path and curl up in the gentle embrace of her verdant motherland. She needed to go home to Wales. She needed the enveloping kindness. She needed to have people on her side. Unconditionally. And above all, she needed the sincerest, warmest, most heart-melting, most protective mark of affection ever invented, that made a mockery of the humdrum hug and blew the air kiss away into an intangible oblivion, she needed the all-encompassing embrace of a Welsh *cwtch*.

The summer holidays were only a week away. It would mark a year since her father's death, which meant that the first anniversary of her separation was also looming. She decided there and then that taking the children back to Wales for the start of the summer holidays would be the best way to deal with all of it. When she came back she would make a new start, get going on a new book, and stop sowing her wild pre-menopausal oats.

In five minutes she'd booked the flights and sent her family a message to say that she was coming home. Not because that's where her heart was, but because she was drawn by some atavistic need to draw from her life source, to take a dip in her own cauldron of magic potion before coming back to fight the Gauls.

CHAPTER 41

They'd slaughtered the wild boar and turned on the taps of mead to mark her return to the old country. Or that's what it felt like at least as she was balloted from one cholesterol-laden teatime trolley of death to another, blown carefree by the winds playfully sending the balls on the cliff-top golf course out to sea and washed free of her continental mannerisms by a good dousing of no-nonsense beer.

Back in her single childhood bed, now that she no longer qualified for the double in the spare bedroom, she felt simultaneously freed of any adult responsibility and burdened with the shame of failure. Her Laura Ashley-branded bedroom was a cruelly conserved reminder of what her dreams of adulthood had been and how they had failed to materialise.

The room that the sign on the door still announced to be the "temporary home of a rising executive" was now only the hideout of a struggling writer. The posters of glamorous buff young pop singers with flicked back, highlighted hair only mocked her current singledom after years of being the wife of a toilet paper salesman, even if his job took him as far as the Pacific Rim. Even her bookshelf, holding her favourite childhood read, "Women in History", chided her that she had done nothing, achieved nothing, had only succeeded in making her marriage history.

On her last morning "home" she'd reverted so far back that she found herself watching Children's BBC and drinking hot chocolate in her pyjamas with Manon and Arthur all morning while her mother hoovered around them. It was no preparation for the looming battle between Boadicea and Joan of Arc but by the time she'd touched down on French soil again, Catherine was ready to unleash her inner dragon.

However, as the taxi they had taken home from the airport turned on its tail, leaving the children and her in front of the house surrounded by their luggage, Catherine slowly realised that the dragon had been expelled from its lair. The remote control wouldn't open the gates. At first she suspected that the battery had gone, and she vented her frustration on the damned domotics but the red light was still coming on with each press of the button, getting angrier and angrier as the gates repeatedly failed to answer its command.

Catherine rummaged in her handbag for the keys to the door-like front gate. Once again her first attack was foiled by an invisible enemy as the key no longer seemed to fit into the lock. It all felt like a bad joke, as if she'd been away for more than a week and returned to another time and place, another dimension where she no longer existed, no longer had any rights.

As she desperately tried to insert the key, checking for a leaf or stone blocking the mechanism, she felt a growing sense of panic, and the children were starting to pick up on it. Arthur needed to use the loo after the long journey and Manon was hungry. She looked around for a solution but the tall hedge with its reinforced wire fence was impenetrable and the spikes that guarded the top of the gates like a troop of Prussian soldiers would leave her pricked like a sausage on a barbecue fork if she attempted to high jump them.

She was barred from her own house.

She took her phone and called Jacques to see whether he knew what was going on. He answered almost at once, as if delectably looking forward to the anticipated phone call. He listened to her describe the situation then calmly gave her the explanation she needed but had not been expecting.

"I've decided to move back in so I've changed the locks. You can't throw me out. You're the one who's breaking up this family. So you can move out. I want the status quo. I'm just a normal family man."

Catherine was lost for words at the idea of being kicked out of the home she had created for her children, at the thought that he'd taken over the keep and raised the drawbridge on her.

"But where am I supposed to go?"

Jacques was heartless in his attack and not content with kicking her out of the castle, held her back with a slew of poisoned arrows.

"That's your problem. Get one of your Facebook friends, one of your Twitter followers, one of your lovers to put you up. Or you have another choice, come home to me as my loyal wife or go home to your own country."

Catherine couldn't hold back her rage.

"But that's just blackmail. Have you really sunk that low? It's as much my home as it is yours. More so, if you think of all my royalties that have gone into it."

But Jacques clearly had a plan in mind and this was only a part of his strategy.

"Let's let the judge decide shall we? I've got the house back and even if I can't get you back, I will get the kids. They were made in France; they were born in France. They are French property."

Catherine's first instinct was to turn around and check that the children were still there. It was unthinkable that he should even consider taking them away from her. He had hardly seen them grow up given that he was away so much, spent so many weekends with his mistress. He was never home and here he was saying that he would ask a judge to give them to him! She couldn't keep her eyes off the children, the only good thing to come out of her marriage, as if making the most of every second in their company. But she was so taken aback that the only argument she could come up with, one that would hardly stand up in court was "But you can't even cook an omelette."

"Don't worry. The house will be bathed in the sweet smell of revenge."

With that he hung up. Revenge? Wasn't she the one who should be out for it? Her husband was clearly in denial about who the baddy was in this story and in his head was joining the establishment in making her the person responsible for breaking up the family. His double life, double-dealing and double faced cheek clearly trumped her single-minded, ingenuous and naïve belief in love and romance.

But it wasn't the time for philosophical musings. She was out in the street with the children. Finding a roof for the night was her first priority.

CHAPTER 42

"Ok kids, just a bit of a problem with the locks, let's continue our holiday at aunty Florence's house. Shall we go and see if she's in?"

Down and out in St Desirée, the three lugged their suitcases the hundred metres or so that separated them from Florence's gated driveway. They had no other choice. Catherine's car was being held hostage in her own garage and even the support she had stocked up on back in Wales was not enough to help her cope with this new obstacle. She needed to see a friendly face.

Catherine had to ring twice before Florence's suspicious "*oui?*" finally came through the interphone.

"You won't believe what he's done now. He's locked me out of my own home."

"But he can't do that to you. It's your house. Didn't your parents buy it for you or something? I'm on my own. David is away, again. But we'll find a solution. Come in for a glass of champagne *chérie*."

Florence was clearly not on the first glass of her panacea, her luxury answer to life's hardships, but the sound of the gate swinging open to let them in was nectar to Catherine's ears.

Helping the children along the long gravel driveway and up the stone steps leading to her stable for the night, Catherine felt a great wave of fatigue wash over her.

But she had another hour of settling into one of Florence's spare bedrooms, of feeding and bathing the children, of putting them into pyjamas and in front of a DVD before she could go back to the kitchen to accept the glass of champagne her friend shoved into her hand, as if she was late joining the party.

"I don't really have any cause for celebration Florence. I don't really see what the occasion is."

Florence had clearly not been spending the last hour cleaning up after dinner or maybe she didn't have the same interpretation of the term 'washing up liquid' even if both contained bubbles.

She looked at Catherine through her glass.

"But *chérie*, champagne is not for celebration. It is to forget. You drink it at weddings to forget that you're going to be cheated on and the more money your husband spends on his mistress the more expensive the champagne you drink. I've ruined him with my Ruinart consumption. And now I'm on Dom Perignon chérie. Obviously not ON him because he was a monk, and he's dead, but you know what I mean. I feel that Kristall isn't too far away either … anyway, enough about me. Tell me, what's going on?"

Catherine told her about returning from her holiday with the children to find she had been evicted from her home. About Jacques' threats to take not only the house but also the children.

"I made it our home, for God's sake I made the children who they are. The only thing he's done is wreck everything."

The story even sobered up Florence, who was rather embarrassed that a fellow countryman could inflict such pain on this poor ingénue who had reckoned that she would be the cultural exception to the French way of life.

"Don't worry. At least you can stay here tonight and for as long as you need to. We'll sort it out in the morning. Things always look better in the morning. I don't, but things do …"

***

Florence's spare room with its en suite guest bathroom felt like a hotel. All it lacked was a minibar. Despite being practically sozzled when they had arrived, she had gone into perfect hostess mode and laid out towels and even a bathrobe on the beds, provided water in beautiful glass decanters on the bedside tables and even brought up her children's old DVDs for the children to watch. But despite the trappings of luxury, Catherine craved only her own familiar bed, her own dressing gown worn into a second skin, her own life.

She found sleep to be as elusive as a husband to a desperate spinster. She would sometimes catch a glimpse of it before it hurried away to take someone else in its arms, leaving her increasingly frustrated and distraught.

After tormented hours of trying not to wake the children with her tossing and turning on a sea of worries and the panic attacks that would leave her gasping for air as if drowning in her own fears, as quietly as she could she got up, opened and closed the bedroom door softly and escaped downstairs to find some solace in her friend's fridge.

She stared rather desolately at its liquid contents, not daring to touch the rather exquisite aperitif pâtés from Dordogne ducks, spreads from Provencal olives and Breton-fished mackerel or the rainbow packs of mini macarons, before deciding to hit the cheeseboard. She carefully removed the heavy glass petri dish of cheeses in different states of melting ooziness and encroaching state of moulding and pushed the door shut with her shoulder.

The scene that followed could easily have been straight out of a Swiss horror film, but she caught the plate of Europe's finest dairy specimens in extremis as it was frightened out of her hands by the black figure that had crept up behind the fridge door. She let out a scream as she backed behind the island ruling the centre of the kitchen and grabbed the vicious-looking cheese knife that had been skulking among the ruins of the Rocamadaour, the splodge of St Marcellin and the sunken cesspool of the Epoisse.

But before she could plunge the knife into her aggressor and send them to a rather cheesy death, Florence's familiar voice emerged from the black masked intruder, which in the dim light coming from the hallway she could now see was a micro fleece skiing balaclava.

"Shush! Are you crazy! It's just me! Florence. I've just had a *fantastique* idea."

Catherine wasn't sure what her friend was on about, but then thought back to her last words before they had turned in.

"But it's not morning yet Florence. And I'm sure you're not that scary."

This time it was Florence's turn to be lost.

"What are you talking about?"

The early hour and the after-effects of Father Perignon's holy water were not helping international understanding and Catherine, already fearing that she had put her foot in it, hesitantly croaked, "Well the balaclava … I thought your idea was to wear it in the morning so you wouldn't…."

Florence finished her sentence for her "… scare the children? Hey I'm not that ugly." But Florence was on too much of a mission to give any further thought to Catherine's rather monumental insult.

"No *mon amie*, we are going to storm the Bastille."

Suddenly Catherine knew perfectly what she was talking about.

"Are you serious? Are you suggesting that we break into the house?"

"*Voila!*" she said like a teacher talking to a child who had just grasped the rudiments of the subjunctive tense in French. "We are going to stage our own 14th of July in reverse and bring back the monarchy by reinstating you on that throne!"

Catherine looked at her friend with a mix of amazement and admiration before reaching for the other black racing mask that Florence was holding in her hand and proclaiming in a loud whisper so as not to wake the children, "Vive la revolution!"

CHAPTER 43

After stopping off in the garage for equipment, a stepladder and a set of tools, the two women set off on their expedition like a rogue neighbourhood watch patrol. At this early hour no cars passed through their residential lane and all the houses were tucked in and snoring behind their thick eiderdowns of cypress hedges.

At Catherine's house, they peeked in at the side of the gates to check that Jacques' car wasn't back. He was away. Whether for business or pleasure or, his time-saving combination of both, who knew.

Looking around one last time, they put the ladder up against the garden hedge and clambered onto its swaying top, using a branch of the laurel bush as a vaulting pole to land on the lawn on the other side. Neither being accomplished athletes, the branches whipped them onto their knees before bouncing back to close ranks and abandoning them in the garden.

As they approached the house, the security lights came on, sending them scurrying to the protection of the dark shadows. They held each other in fear as an owl hooted, but as soon as the lights timed out they continued to skim the walls to make their way around to the kitchen window.

Florence was proving to have more DIY skills than Catherine would have given her credit for and wielded the screwdriver with the agility of a conductor and the speed of an electric whisk as she got going on dismantling the closed wooden shutters. But the rust had sealed the screws into place and it took a chisel and elbow grease to hack at the wood and prise open a space wide enough to put a hand in to lift the latch.

The window was now laid bare before them, their faces reflected in its dark pool. Florence then ceremoniously handed Catherine the hammer from the tool box with the words, "I'll leave the honours to you."

Catherine wasn't sure what was honourable about smashing her way into her own home but took the proffered instrument anyway. She wasn't committing any crime, if she wanted to break a window in her own home, she could, but Florence on the other hand could be done for not-so-common burglary.

Sizing up the window and weighing the hammer in her hand, Catherine then lifted it above her head and brought it down on the glass. Nothing. Not even a crack.

The two women looked at each other.

"Good quality," Florence said without a hint of irony.

Catherine drew on her anger and frustration and injected it into her second attempt. With a noise that she imagined could be heard throughout the village, the slivers of glass rained down on the work surface inside and slid like a waterfall onto the floor.

The next step was to get through the window. Both women started to painstakingly remove the shards that were still sticking out of the putty in the frames and that would lacerate them like a torturous ruff were they to put their heads through it.

After a few minutes of this clearing operation Catherine gave Florence an embarrassed nudge and simply put her hand through the defiled window to turn the handle from the inside and open the two panes in full.

Florence looked at her.

"We won't mention that to anyone, ok?"

Catherine nodded at her seriously at the thought that she had lived up to her blondness but then both broke out into a hushed giggling fit.

They pushed the windows open as far as they would go and hoisted themselves up to the windowsill and over the window frame, their small step for womankind ending up in the kitchen sink.

As soon as they had forded the pool of glass on the floor, they stopped for a moment to listen out for any sounds coming from inside the house or from the street outside before turning on the light.

Catherine was firing on all cylinders, "So what now?" she eagerly asked her friend.

But Florence hadn't really thought any further than getting her friend back inside the house. Improvising, she opened the fridge and announced "I think we should just celebrate the moral victory," and took out a bottle of champagne.

Also at a loss to know what she could gain from her advantage, from reclaiming her property, Catherine simply sat down beside her on the floor and, between swigs of ethereal bubbles, toasted their rather hollow achievement.

"But hey, seriously, what do I do now?"

Florence looked at her earnestly.

"You fight. You fight for the children. You fight for your home. You fight for yourself. The fun and games end here. You stop playtime and go to court."

Catherine felt increasingly out of control of her own life. She turned to her friend again as if she was a clairvoyant who could reassure her of the outcome.

"And how does it end? Will there be a happy ending?"

"You're the writer chérie. It's up to you to write it that way. Come on, let's start by patching up this window in case some real burglars come in and then you can start patching up your life."

But Catherine only wanted to go back to the children, who were peacefully asleep back at Florence's. She quickly did a quick tour of the house, packing clothes and her computer into canvas shopping bags along the way. They walked out of the front door, Jacques having left the key of the changed lock on the inside to block anyone coming in from the outside. As Catherine turned around to lock in her past, she was determined that, the next time, she would return with her head held high. With a final click, the house was returned to its museum-like silence, containing only the dusty artefacts of her married past.

EPILOGUE

Back in Florence's house, she climbed into bed next to the children with her laptop and began writing. It started off as a classic-ish fairy tale:

"Once upon a time there was an innocent and optimistic young girl who, after working her way through a pond of German beer, ended up kissing a frog. Carried away by the potent effects of the potion and the dizzying highs of freedom, the creature turned into a prince before her eyes. After a white wedding in an enchanted castle, two perfect children, followed by years of seeing her prince hop further and further away from her, from one lily pad to another, she realised that the frog had, in fact, been a poisonous, hallucination-inducing toad and the prince only a figment of love's naïve young dream, a will-o'-the-wisp she had followed over the water before losing her way as the light went out. In fact, the frog had always remained a frog. The young girl decided to throw the slimy green amphibian with its cleft tongue back into the pond and so they divorced and lived separately ever after.

The End

How definitive those two words sounded. And yet she had no ending, no conclusion, no psychologically-satisfying closure. Her past was something she no longer trusted, it hadn't been real, only a figment of her imagination. The pond had been a cesspit and she would now have to wash their dirty linen, the lipstick-stained collars and semen-smeared 'why-oh-why?-fronts" in it and hang them up in a divorce court to dry, in public.

To get the dirt she would have to delve deep into the murky past until the tears of hurt streamed as she hit upon the rockiness of their relationship, pick at the scabs until the blood ran, and dissect the bloody corpse of their love in a post mortem of their marriage.

From the last phone call, she knew that her husband would do everything to arise from the coffin she had crafted for him. To crawl out from the grave he had dug for himself. No, the battle ahead was to be no cautionary fairy tale or moralistic fable. Not even a fantastic tale of the undead. It was set to be a Greek tragedy.

This time when she looked back, it wouldn't be to invite him over a few pints of ambrosia to the Elysium she had to offer him. No, she would look Jacques defiantly in the face and send him back to Hades, where he belonged. After all, he obviously knew his way around the nether regions pretty well.

At the same time, she knew that he was going to do everything in his power to drag her down to the underworld with him. But that was a risk she was willing to take. What could be the worst he could do to her?

She was soon to find out what the bilingual dictionaries diplomatically didn't tell you. She would discover for herself the nuance they omitted from their rather literal translation.

She would experience at first hand that "hell" was the French for divorce.

THE END

Made in the USA
Charleston, SC
14 February 2017